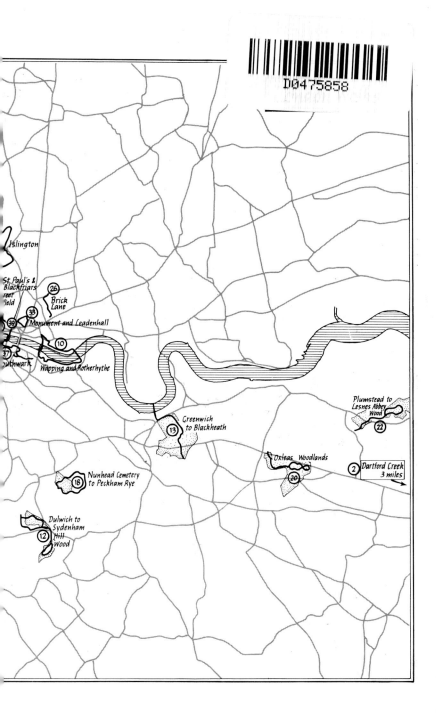

Islington

St Paul's &
Blackfriars
reet
field

26 Brick
Lane

33

39 Monument and Leadenhall

37 10

uthwark

Wapping and Rotherhythe

13 Greenwich
to Blackheath

Plumstead to
Lesnes Abbey
Wood

22

18 Nunhead Cemetery
to Peckham Rye

Oxleas Woodlands

20

2 Dartford Creek
3 miles

12 Dulwich to
Sydenham
Hill
Wood

D0475858

London Walks

London Walks

Tiffany Daneff

with photographs by
Peter Ryan

Michael Joseph
London

For Mama

MICHAEL JOSEPH LTD
Published by the Penguin Group
27 Wrights Lane, London W8 5TZ, England
Viking Penguin Inc., 40 West 23rd Street, New York, New York 10010, USA
Penguin Books Australia Ltd, Ringwood, Victoria, Australia
Penguin Books Canada Ltd, 2801 John Street, Markham, Ontario, Canada L3R 1B4
Penguin Books (NZ) Ltd, 182–190 Wairau Road, Auckland 10, New Zealand

Penguin Books Ltd, Registered Offices, Harmondsworth, Middlesex, England

First published in Great Britain in 1989

Text copyright © Tiffany Daneff 1989
Photographs copyright © Peter Ryan 1989
Maps by Neil Hyslop
The quotation on page 8 is reprinted
by permission of Faber and Faber Ltd from
Four Quartets by T. S. Eliot
Title page: Chestnut Tree Avenue in Holland Park

Typeset in 10/12 pt Ehrhardt by Wilmaset, Birkenhead, Wirral
Printed and bound in Great Britain by Butler & Tanner Ltd, Frome

A CIP catalogue record for this book is available
from the British Library

ISBN 0 7181 3116 9

Library of Congress 89–80134

Contents

Foreword

Londoners can take London for granted. There's so much to see and to know that it's difficult to take it all in. Crushed in a stale underground compartment hurtling around the Circle Line, it's easy to forget the tranquillity of walking beside the river early in the morning when the mist has not yet lifted; or of leaving the first footprints on the dew-drunk grass of Kensington Gardens – dew which is as fresh as that which falls on the Orkneys.

This isn't a book for Londoners only, but for visitors and tourists too. There are walks around the more famous sights, many of which I had not seen since my childhood, and enjoyed far more than I, a blasé Londoner, had expected. There are walks beside the rivers and canals that afford a home to much of the city's wildlife; walks in the seventy square miles of parks, meadows and public gardens in Greater London; plus a few excursions.

In going on these walks, I have been as excited as any explorer. Discovering pockets of ancient woodland, like Sydenham Hill Wood, now cared for by the London Wildlife Trust, or the abandoned plain of the River Darent in Dartford, now threatened with development, has been as rewarding as an expedition to a new country. I started to notice the details – a terracotta cow's head stuck on the wall above a newsagent's shop near the World's End, the extraordinary variety of window decoration – and found that every street told its own story. I hope you get as much pleasure out of doing these walks as I have.

Tiffany Daneff
Notting Hill Gate 1988

Note on the Routes

The maps and textual routes are as detailed as possible, but I advise you to check a London A-Z street guide before setting out and, if possible, have one handy as you walk (especially for the street walks).

At the beginning of each walk I have listed the nearest bus, underground and British Rail stations, although I usually drove to the start of the walks. I have left getting back up to you.

We shall not cease from exploration
And the end of all our exploring
Will be to arrive where we started
And know the place for the first time.

Little Gidding, T. S. Eliot

WATERSIDE WALKS

1 Camden Lock

Length: just over 2 miles there and back. Good for push- or wheelchairs. Food: cafés, restaurants and snacks at Camden Lock and in Camden High Street. Canal boat trips: The London Waterbus Company (tel. 01–482–2550) daily and hourly from March to October and every 1½ hours at weekends during the winter. Jason's Trip provides a similar service on a traditional barge (tel. 01–286–3428). Bus: No. 74.

This walk takes little more than half an hour and is a particularly good one to do with children as there is plenty to look at and if they get tired you can take a barge back. To extend the walk, either join the canal at Little Venice (page 34) or continue walking eastwards to St Pancras Lock and Camley Street Natural Park.

The canal towpath can be joined at several points along Prince Albert Road, but Macclesfield Bridge is by the bus stop. In summer the banks are thick with cow parsley and the trees on the edge of Regent's Park colour the water green. There are footbridges if you want to cross over to the park which dates back, like so many of London's green spaces, to Henry VIII who seized what was then woodland from the Manor of Tyburn and Abbess of Barking and turned it into a deer park, known as Marylebone Park. Cromwell sold the park to individuals who made a quick profit by cutting down most of the trees. The present park was designed by John Nash as a neo-classical garden with lake and formal flower gardens.

After the second footbridge the towpath passes below the wire tent of the Snowdon aviary filled with birds like the red-billed whistling duck and the cattle egret. A noticeboard at towpath level tells you all about them. On the other side of the canal you can see the deer and buffalo.

The Regent's Canal was the idea of Thomas Homer, a London businessman who realised the potential of linking the Grand Junction Canal at Paddington Basin to the Docks. Homer met Nash who was delighted to incorporate the canal into the plans for his park.

It took eight years to build the eight-and-a-half-mile cut through the fields as work was continually beset with problems. When it

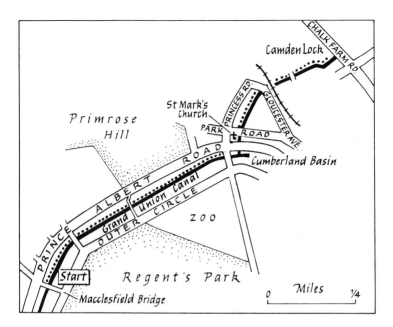

finally opened in 1820, companies enthusiastically switched from land to water transport. Success was short-lived. In 1837 Euston station was opened and by the 1870s the waterways were losing cargoes to the railways. The Regent's Canal survived for longer than rural canals as it handled the explosives and building materials needed for the massive expansion of London. But by the end of the century the railways had evidently won.

Canals were nationalised in 1948 and the Regent's Canal was abandoned until the 1970s when the Central Electricity Generating Board laid six 400-kilowatt cables under the towpath and covered them with concrete. In this somewhat sinister way the canal has been preserved.

After passing the zoo you reach the Cumberland Basin where several traditionally painted barges are moored. The canal then turns left and north past a row of individual Georgian villas with gardens sweeping down to the eastern bank. Sycamore, elm, birch and ash trees and wildflowers grow beside the path. These disappear as you approach the Southampton Bridge pumping station, disguised as a fort and part of which – the Pirate's Castle – is used as a children's canoeing centre.

The Grand Union Canal from Camden Lock

Soon you reach warehouses where the towpath climbs a cobbled bridge. The lock is now below you. To the left, through a narrow archway in the wall, the buildings around the basin have been transformed into workshops, stalls and cafés. Stalls selling clothes, toys, bric-a-brac, antiques and fashion are spread out over the cobbles amongst street entertainers.

Beside the lock is the canal information centre. Continuing under Chalk Farm Road, on the left-hand side of the canal, you pass the TV-am Breakfast Television studios. The canal continues through rough industrial landscape to St Pancras. At Camden Lock there are regular barges back to Regent's Park and Little Venice.

2 Dartford Creek

Length: about 7 miles. Don't go
alone, as it is deserted. Don't take
wheel- or pushchairs. Food: The
Huffler in Hythe Lane. Buses:
Nos LC400 and Green Line 472
and 725. British Rail: Dartford.

The flood plain of the River Darent has the listless air of the
unemployed, but it wasn't always so. From Elizabethan days when
there were four wharfs on the river and several paper mills, the river
worked for a living. By the 1830s, 55,000 tons of cargo a year came to
Dartford by barge, the largest barges mooring halfway up the creek
and transferring their load on to smaller boats. Until the 1960s there
were munitions factories here but they were closed after flooding in
1953 when the water reached eight feet on the flood plain.

By the black weatherboarded cottage in Hythe Street, a narrow
alleyway leads to a mossy wooden footbridge over shiny green mud in
the creek. Following the path you reach a solitary lock cottage
surrounded by allotments with small green cabbages and bright red
dahlias. Past the lock, the path rises to an embankment opposite the
Wiggins Teape paper factory which pollutes the river with soap-
powder-blue effluent.

Standing on the embankment you can see the concrete flood
barrier marking the position of the Thames. Beside the levee, black
and white cows pasture amongst wild rose briars, and an absurd
crowd of farm geese and wild Canada geese skedaddle across a
ploughed field. You can see farm buildings to the east.

This is a lonely place, but beautiful. If Kent County Council has
its way, the flood plain will soon disappear when bulldozers and
cranes arrive to carve into the soft brown earth and pour on liquid
cement, turning it into the Dartford Northern Bypass.

Further on muddy bullrushes sway with the incoming tide, the
water lapping against the rotting wood of a wrecked barge, bow
tipped in the mud. High above a skylark flits and dips, trilling loudly.
Snipe, heron and a flock of tern and plover wade in the river and
plouter about in the mud.

In spring the embankment is thick with tansy, red and white clover
and yellow crowsfoot. Ox-eye daisies cover the slopes like white

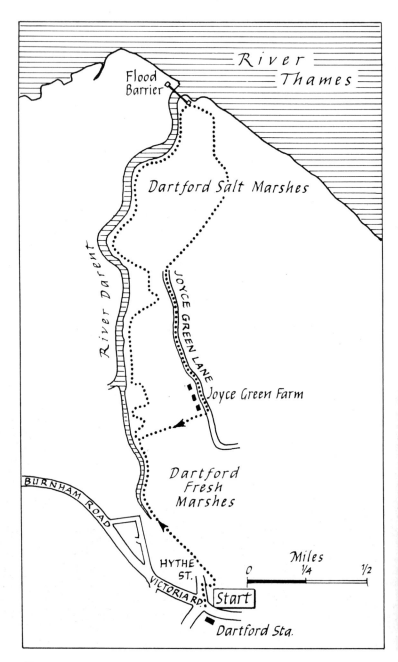

sheets and tiny common blue butterflies flutter about the single dark pink flower of the grass vetchling.

On the skyline, a large container barge moves across the fields like a cow. The Thames is invisible until you get quite close. On the opposite bank you can see the cement works at Purfleet. The gravelled levee leads to a copse below the towers of Littlebrook power station where a rough track through trees leads to the Dartford salt marshes. The joyless building ahead was the Joyce Green Isolation Hospital which was closed in 1977 and deliberately set on fire to remove all traces of disease.

The salt marshes are like a dry primeval bog, springy to the step and on close inspection covered in tiny green growth. Following an old country road past the disused Unwins pyrotechnics factory, you pass the old signs warning trespassers they will be fined £5. Inside the factory walls are the individual corrugated iron shacks the explosives were made in, to avoid the whole lot going up in one almighty blast.

When you come to the brick-walled farm buildings on the right (the Joyce Green farm), take the turning just before the modern bungalow at the end, asking permission from the farmer first, and follow the farm track back to the creek.

Ox-eye daisies beside the River Darent

3 Bishop's Park River Walk

Length: 6½ miles there and back. Good for push- or wheelchairs. Food: the Odd Spot café in Crisp Road is open Mon–Sat 7 a.m.–5 p.m; The Blue Anchor Rutland Ale House in the Lower Mall and The Dove in Upper Mall. There's a good toddler's playground in Bishop's Park. Buses to Putney Bridge 14, 22, 30, 39, 74, 80, 85, 93, 220, 264; from the Great West Road 290, E3. Underground: Putney Bridge.

At the end of Bishop's Avenue enter the large iron gates. A small Victorian lodge, decorated with barley sugar chimneys, squats at the entrance to Bishop's Palace, the official residence of the Bishops of London from the eleventh century until 1973. Through an arch in the high red-brick wall you reach the entrance to the Fitzjames Quadrangle, the oldest part of the palace, built by Bishop Fitzjames at the beginning of the sixteenth century. Small mullioned windows peer over the courtyard, in the middle of which splashes a fountain.

The view of the palace from the riverside gives a totally different impression. Lawns lead to a well-proportioned early nineteenth-century stucco front and, to the left, a red sandstone chapel, built in 1867. At the end of the lawns, a wrought-iron gate in a moss-covered, crumbly wall, leads through to the Elizabethan Herbarium, best seen in late spring and early summer when the herbs grow up above the lozenge-shaped box hedge parterre. A lovely crusty wistaria climbs round the garden separating it from the old kitchen garden.

Walking from the palace grounds to the river, turn right and walk under the avenue of plane trees towards Craven Cottage football ground. Craven Cottage was a rural retreat built by the 6th Baron Craven in 1785 for his wife. The fun-loving Baroness got bored, and fled to the Continent where she met and married the Margrave of Brandenburg-Ansbach. Returning to Fulham they settled in Brandenburg House which quickly became the centre of fashionable society. The Margravine was however never accepted at Court because she had lived with her second husband whilst the first was still alive. Craven Cottage, a rather pretty house with dormer

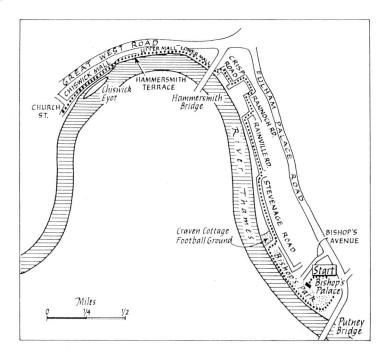

windows and probably a thatched roof, was leased by the Bishop of London to a succession of tenants. In 1888 the cottage was destroyed by fire and fifteen years later the land was bought by Fulham Football Club.

The next section of the riverside walk has been built quite recently with help from Shell UK, whose vast barges unload petrol here into three huge storage tanks. Disused depots have been removed and their containers variously converted into a football pitch, slides and a small garden.

A narrow passage leads to the modern Crabtree Tavern and the Watneys-sponsored section of the walk. On a small shingle beach a Canada goose, shelduck and moorhen pick amongst the jetsam and red sorrel below a solitary willow. Away from the river the landscape is changing fast. Humble brick and stucco Victorian terraces end abruptly in a modern development. Palace Wharf, an imposing Victorian warehouse, has been converted by Richard Rogers and now houses the architect's offices. The Riverside Studios in Crisp Road put on art exhibitions and shows and have a good bookshop.

Flood tide, Chiswick Mall

Turn left out of Crisp Road into River Terrace and walk through the gardens to the Lower Mall which continues under the vast ironwork of Hammersmith Bridge, built in 1883–7 by Joseph Bazalgette. Pale wistaria and faded roses tumble over the elegant eighteenth-century cottages overlooking the river. Behind the river wall, barges and rafts rattle and clank with the ebb and flow. A traditional sailing barge is moored beside the Dove Marina, on the site of Hammersmith Creek, where boats of 200 tons discharged their cargoes in Hammersmith harbour until 1921.

In the narrow alley leading to Upper Mall is the famous Dove Inn, licensed for four hundred years, though the present building dates from the eighteenth century. James Thomson is supposed to have written the words to 'Rule Britannia' sitting in the old coffee house. Kelmscott House, at the end of the alley on the right, was built in the 1780s. A blue plaque on the wall commemorates Francis Ronalds who invented the electric cable here in 1816, laying eight miles of it in the garden. The novelist and poet George Macdonald lived here from 1867–77 and then let it to William Morris who lived here until his death.

18

When Hammersmith Terrace was built in 1755, these tall brick town houses with their proud Doric porches were surrounded by fields and market gardens. The terrace leads to Chiswick Mall where grand eighteenth- and nineteenth-century mansions overlook pretty riverside gardens beside Chiswick Eyot. Morton House and Strawberry House were built in 1730. Walpole House was started in the sixteenth century and has seventeenth-century additions. It became a school in the nineteenth century which William Thackeray attended and which may be the model for Miss Pinkerton's Academy in *Vanity Fair*.

The worn brick walls in front of the houses are covered with old-fashioned flowers and across the road, which is liable to flooding, are lovely rose-trellised gardens leading to the river's edge. St Nicholas's Church, which stands near the site of the old ford, has a fifteenth-century ragstone tower. The body of the church was rebuilt in 1882 and an urn in the graveyard is dedicated to William Hogarth who lived close by in Hogarth House. You can either turn round and walk back or catch a bus back from the Great West Road.

4 Islington

Length: about 4 miles. Good for push- and wheel-chairs. Food: The Marquess Tavern in Willow Bridge Road; The Crown or The Albion in Cloudesley Road. Buses: Nos 4, 19, 30, 43, 263A, 279, 279A. Underground: Angel.

Leaving the Angel underground station, turn right into Upper Street and walk round the bend to reach the cobbled entrance to Islington High Street leading to Camden Passage. The two-storey Georgian houses in Camden Passage lean close together over old York paving stones and on market days (Monday to Saturday) the passage is lined with stalls selling antiques, bric-a-brac, secondhand paperbacks etc.

Passing Duncan Street, continue along the Passage to Charlton Place and turn right along a one-sided crescent of late eighteenth-century town houses. No. 15 on the other side of the street is a lovely three-bay early Georgian house. The two bow-fronted end terrace houses in Duncan Terrace form a neck at the end of Charlton Place.

Leaving Charlton Place, walk up the steps on the right on to Duncan Terrace, built in 1768. Charles Lamb lived at No. 64. Below the wide paved terrace runs a narrow strip of garden. Walk along the raised terrace and down the steps at the other end to cross into the garden opposite the red-brick church of St John the Evangelist. At the end of the gardens cross Colebrooke Row and walk through the entrance in the railings at the corner of Vincent Terrace to walk down the steps that join the towpath beside the Grand Union Canal.

The canal emerges from the dark tunnel that has brought it here from Caledonian Road and flows sluggishly past the traditionally painted canal boats. The roses and creepers from the opposite gardens trail down the brick wall behind a row of anglers.

At the Danbury Street bridge you have to walk up some steps, cross the bridge and continue along the towpath on the other side of the canal. Slabs of marble and sacks of plaster are piled up outside Harris Wharf, an imposing Victorian building, still in use. Two rusty Thames sailing barges are slowly fed through City Road Lock by a

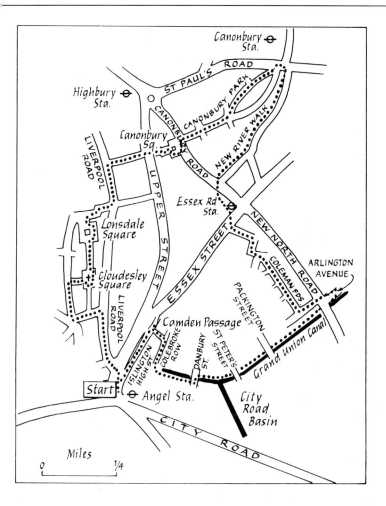

tough tug boat. The warehouses on the other side of City Road Basin have already been turned into offices.

Walking underneath Wharf Road you reach a canalside entrance to The Narrow Boat pub. Continuing beside the canal, now almost twice its previous width, you pass more canal boats, a playground on the left and a factory on the right. It is not particularly pretty but it is interesting. The next bridge leads on to a second lock.

Immediately after the next bridge, take the stairs up to Baring Street. Cross over the busy New North Road and continue along

Arlington Avenue into the spacious Arlington Square estate, built in the 1840s and allowing twice the usual road width. Turn right into Arlington Square and continue along Coleman Fields crossing Linton and St Paul Streets.

At the junction with Basire Street, turn left and right, walking through the council estate to Greenman Street which contains the pub of the same name and a few fruit, vegetable and flower stalls. Turning right into Essex Road, cross it (it is busy) and turn left into River Place to reach Canonbury Grove and the beginning of the New River Walk.

The story of the New River goes back to the early 1600s when London, with a surging population of 300,000, outgrew its thirteenth-century conduits. The Thames was so foul that in 1570 Parliament ordered a new river to be dug to bring fresh water from the springs of Chadwell and Amwell in Hertfordshire to North London.

By September 1613, the ten-foot wide New River had reached its destination thirty-eight miles later in the old Ducking Pond behind Sadler's Wells. The New River now ends at Stoke Newington where the two reservoirs and their wildlife are currently under threat of development by Thames Water.

The length of river along Canonbury Grove has been preserved as a walk. The small round hut near the entrance is often thought to be Jacobean but is more likely to be a nineteenth-century linesman's hut. The lovely houses on the right in Canonbury Grove were built in the 1820s when Canonbury developed from a rural village to a London suburb.

At the exit on to Willow Bridge Road, turn left over the bridge and continue along the river walk through the iron gate on the bridge. On the right is the Marquess Tavern. The brackish water is a black reflection of the former river. With the flowerbeds and shrubs, ducks, benches and a wooden bridge it's not unlike a willow-pattern plate.

At the end of the river, leave by the gate and turn left into Canonbury Park North where there are some fine detached houses. Continuing into Canonbury Place you pass a uniform row of two-tone brick local shops. Beyond these is Canonbury Tower, a red-brick building dominated by a square tower. It stands on a pre-Roman base and is supposed to have twenty-four ley lines passing through it. It was originally built by the last Prior of St Bartholo-

New River Walk

mew's, William Bolton, before the Priory was dissolved and the Manor given away. It has since been added to and restored.

From here walk round the Georgian terraces in Canonbury Square and cross Upper Street, which is quite busy, into Islington Park Street. Turn left at the junction with Liverpool Road, whose top end was bordered with market gardens until the 1820s. This is an attractive but busy main road. Take the third turning on the right into Barnsbury Street and left into Thornhill Road. Walk through Lonsdale and Cloudesley Squares into Cloudesley Road. This estate was built during the 1820s on land known as 'the Stoney Field, otherwise the Fourteen Acres', bequeathed to Islington by Richard Cloudesley in 1517. From these peaceful leafy village streets turn left to Liverpool Road and the Angel underground station.

5 Kew Towpath and Gardens

Length: just over $4\frac{1}{2}$ miles. Bumpy but fair going for wheel- and pushchairs – could be muddy. Kew Gardens are open daily from 10.00 a.m. to 4.00 p.m. in winter or 8.00 p.m. in summer. Kew Palace is open daily April to September; for details tel. 01–940–3321. Buses: Nos 27, 65 (Sundays No. 7). Underground: Kew Gardens. British Rail: Kew Bridge.

To reach the towpath head down Ferry Lane to the right of Kew Gardens main gates. The river is shored up with stone embankments and hardened bags of cement dividing the pebbled foreshore from the grassy path. On the other side of the river, past the crumbling mudflats of Brentford Docks and the new Brentford Marina, are the parklands of Syon House. The river sighs and lets itself go, loosening its tight metropolitan girdle to lick the roots of willows and alders and lap the bald mud.

Five grey herons perch in the low boughs, swooping for fish, spreading their paddle-like wings and flying up to a large, untidy nest knotted high in the trees. At low tide treasure-hunters come and let their Geiger counters hover over the mud. Prehistoric and Saxon finds have been made here and a Roman hut was excavated on the northern foreshore in 1928.

What looks like a moat dividing Kew Gardens from the towpath is the ha-ha built in 1767 to stop cows from straying. Suddenly Syon House appears through the trees, a great rectangle of pale yellow stone. The towpath curves east with the river, passing the boundary of Kew Gardens to continue alongside the Old Deer Park. A shadow passes over the path as it enters a small copse. The high embankment disappears for a while and the trees at the edge of the foreshore flutter like muddy washing lines hung with assorted plastics.

The towpath continues to Richmond Bridge. Retracing your steps opposite Isleworth Ait you have to walk past the Isleworth Ferry Gate (which is closed) and back to Brentford Ferry Gate in the corner of the car park to enter Kew Gardens.

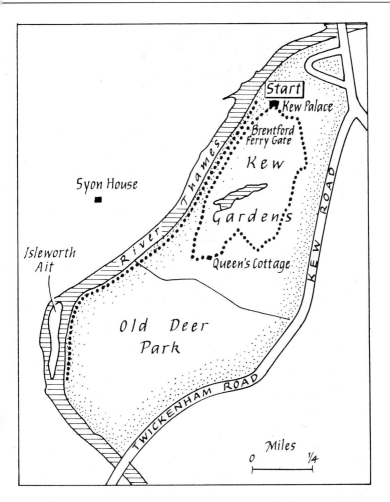

Kew Palace is on the left as you go through the gates. This distinctive dark red-brick house with Dutch gables, originally known as the Dutch House, was built in 1631 for a merchant, Samuel Fortrey. Queen Caroline leased it in 1728 for ninety-nine years, and it became George II's favourite home.

Augusta, the Dowager Princess of Wales, started a botanic garden on nine acres of land south of the Orangery in 1759. With the help of William Aiton, head gardener, William Chambers, architect and Joseph Banks, who became director, Kew Gardens flourished. Thirty years later, 5,500 different species were growing in the

gardens, now enlarged to more than a hundred acres. The well-dressed public, often arriving by river, were allowed in on Thursdays to wander amongst the wooded walks.

Behind the palace are the Queen's Gardens, opened by Queen Elizabeth II in 1969. They're laid out like a formal seventeenth-century garden with herbs and medicinal plants each marked with a quote from Gerard's *Herbal* (compiled in 1597).

Coming out of the palace grounds, turn towards the Thames and follow Riverside Avenue, a clipped grass path between the long grass and great oaks. In the clearing at the end of the avenue stands a massive atlas cedar; its branches sweep across the grass as if to clasp the world and Syon House across the water.

Queen Charlotte's Cottage grounds, carpeted with bluebells in May, were left to the public by Queen Victoria in 1899 on her Diamond Jubilee on condition that they remained in their semi-natural state. When the thatched cottage appears on the left, look out on the right for some witch-hazel bushes. The cottage, built in 1772 as a picnic place for Queen Charlotte, is charming and takes little time to see. Children love it. There are rows of Hogarths downstairs and painted floral ceilings upstairs.

Walking east through Japanese cedars to the Cedar Vista you can see the famous red and black pagoda, built for Princess Augusta in 1761–2 by William Chambers. Unfortunately you can't go up it. The path on the left leads to the Temperate House, a palace for plants. The main part was built in 1860–2, and the two wings in 1895–9 by architect Decimus Burton and builder/ironmaster Richard Turner, who was responsible for the beautiful ironwork that curls up to the sky and spans the great panes of glass above.

By contrast the new Conservatory, opened by the Princess of Wales in 1987, is composed of frosted glass angles and has a clinical air. This, the most sophisticated greenhouse in the world, with computer-controlled heating and ventilation, has more to do with function than style.

Kew Towpath, south of the gardens

6 Petersham

Length: just over 2½ miles. Not recommended for wheel- or push-chairs. Food: Dysart Arms in Petersham High Street. Bus: Nos 65, 71. British Rail: Richmond.

Petersham is still very much a riverside village although the high street has to cope with a lot of traffic to and from London. From the bottom of Richmond Hill, climb past a row of distinguished eighteenth-century red-brick and stucco houses on the left. On the right there is a gravelled viewpoint, with a telescope, where you can watch the Thames curve in a great bow towards Windsor. You can see the Terrace Gardens below, which you get into through the gate you passed coming up the hill. The gardens descend towards the river in a series of paths, flowering shrubs and green lawns with flowerbeds as neat as pastry cuts.

Walk through the gardens, keeping parallel with the Thames. As you leave the gardens, cross over the path that leads up on the left to a flight of worn stone steps and bent white iron railings. Don't go up them; instead, walk straight ahead over Terrace Field, a rough field full of clumps of grass. Cross over Nightingale Lane and head to a small, untidy wood behind a large red-brick building, the Star and Garter Home for disabled soldiers. This massive lump, dominating the Hill, replaced the famous eighteenth-century inn of the same name, described at the time as 'more like the mansion of a nobleman than a receptacle for the public'. Louis-Philippe stayed here on his flight from France and Dickens celebrated his wedding anniversary here with an annual dinner party.

There are several well-trodden leaf tracks through Petersham Common wood leading to the junction with Petersham Road and Star and Garter Hill. Follow Petersham Road to the village, considered two hundred years ago to be the prettiest in England. Exceptionally lovely houses front the high street. Petersham Lodge, the most famous of these, stood beside the Dysart Arms and was knocked down a hundred and fifty years ago. The present Lodge, in River Lane, is the imposing white house, visible from Richmond

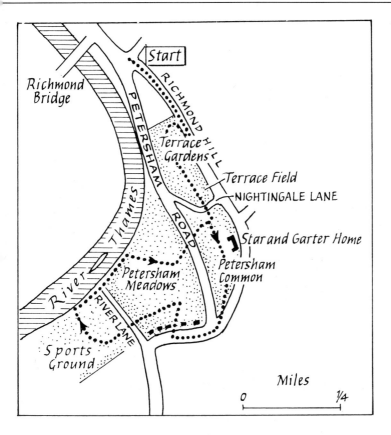

Hill. It was built in 1740, with subsequent extensions, for Robert Ord, Chief Baron of the Exchequer of Scotland.

Just after the Dysart Arms, a footpath on the right leads to the rural eighteenth-century parish church of St Peter's. Captain George Vancouver, discoverer of Vancouver Island, lies buried in the small graveyard at the back. Looking over the low hedge you can see across the meadows to the Thames and up to Richmond Hill.

Returning to the footpath, continue towards the river, turning left off it into a narrow alley, barely a yard's width. This runs parallel with the main street, between gardens and brick walls. Cross the tarmac road, River Lane, and continue walking to Douglas House. Turn right by the stables along a rough track past a sports field. It can be boggy as you get near the river. Turn right on to the towpath and walk past the end of River Lane. When you reach Petersham

The Thames from Richmond Hill

Meadows, which might have cattle or sheep grazing in them, head over the fields towards the Star and Garter which you can see clearly above you. Cross Petersham Road and follow the track up the hill which brings you to the top of Richmond Hill to the right of Nightingale Lane. Turning left to walk down the hill you pass Wick House, built by William Chambers for Joshua Reynolds in 1772. Next to it is The Wick, a neo-classical brick house built in 1775.

7 Putney Towpath and Barnes

Length: 4 miles round trip. Rough going though possible for push-chairs. Food: The Star and Garter at Putney; the Sun Inn, Barnes Green. Barn Elms Reservoirs: details available from Thames Water, tel. 01–837–3300 ext. 6257. Buses: Nos 14, 22, 30, 80, 85, 93, 220, 264. Underground: Putney Bridge.

Turn left out of Putney Bridge station and cross the bridge. Turn right into Lower Richmond Road and leaving Putney Bridge, bear right down towards the river by the Star and Garter on to the Embankment, past boathouses, boatclubs and varnished rowing boats stacked on top of each other.

The walk begins at the end of the road where a small bridge leads over Beverley Brook which has flowed through Richmond Park, Wimbledon and Barnes to the beginning of the towpath. Ash, hawthorn, alder and willows lean over the river. At high tide the tea-brown Thames laps the top of the embankment. The skinny grey alders are left with milky rings by the ebbing tide. At low tide you can climb down and walk along the pebbled foreshore or sit on the boat ramps and stare over the water to Bishop's Park (page 16).

After Barn Elms playing fields, once part of the manor of Francis Walsingham, Elizabeth I's Secretary of State, you pass a high grassy embankment. Behind this lie the Barn Elms Reservoirs. As many as 20,000 gulls have been counted on the 86½ acres of reservoirs in January and there have been sightings of cormorant, green- and redshank, great-crested grebe, heron and over twenty other rare birds. Walking along the towpath one is more likely to see finch, blue tit, wren and duck.

In front of the reservoirs stands a centenary memorial to Steve Fairbairn (1862–1938), oarsman and coach-founder of the Head of the River Race. He was also the father-in-law of the glamorous post-war socialite, Nancy Cunard. Fairbairn's memorial stands a mile from the start of the University Boat Race.

A massive blackened terracotta building dominates the next

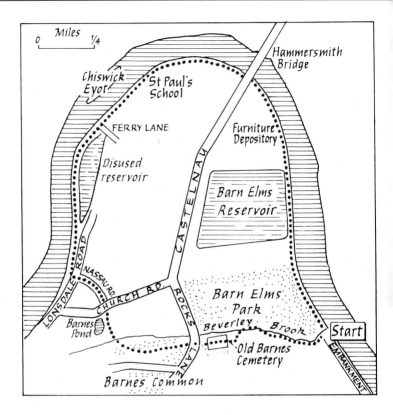

section of the walk. This is Harrods' Furniture Depository, its flags flying like some medieval castle. In front of it is an overgrown wharf where a light railway took furniture to and from the depository. Victorian wharfs lead up to Hammersmith Bridge, built by Joseph Bazalgette in 1887 to replace the Thames' first suspension bridge.

Round the bend in the river, opposite St Paul's Boys' School and playing fields, Chiswick Eyot bristles yellow with dry rushes and pollarded willows after the summer. It divides Chiswick and Corney Reaches where the river broadens and tugs still deliver cargoes to the warehouses on the opposite bank. Coming into sight round the next corner is the black, triple-humped silhouette of Barnes railway bridge, built in 1849 by Joseph Locke.

If you want to shorten the walk turn back where you see the earthy track on the left to walk past a disused reservoir to rejoin the towpath opposite Chiswick Eyot.

Putney Towpath, east of Barn Elms reservoir

The footpath joins Lonsdale Road which you cross to turn down Nassau Road. At Church Road, cross to Barnes Pond. This is a small village pond surrounded by wooden benches and willows, local shops and schools. At the far end of Barnes Green a footbridge crosses on to Barnes Common, over Beverley Brook which runs along the back wall of a terrace of private gardens. The brook is shallow and pebbled, overhung with willows and surrounded by ivy. Although Barnes Common was drained at the end of the last century it can still be very boggy, though not as treacherous as the marsh it once was. It's fertile soil, attracting a large number of plants and creatures, and has been designated a Site of Special Scientific Interest.

As the common land rises towards Rocks Lane, and the grass becomes rough and tussocky, the path leads past oak and thorn to Old Barnes Cemetery. There are several tracks worn through the small, overgrown cemetery. At the other end of the cemetery head left across the fields down to Beverley Brook. Cross the bridge towards the playing fields and turn right to follow the path beside the brook back to the Thames.

8 Little Venice to Wormwood Scrubs

Length: 5 miles there and back. Fine for push- and wheelchairs. Food: pubs in Delamere Road and at various points along the canal. Buses: Nos 6, 16, 18, 36, 36B. Underground: Warwick Avenue.

This walk follows the towpath along the Grand Union Canal from the basin at Little Venice to the junction with Scrubs Lane. The canal was opened in 1814 in the great canal-building period. By the turn of the century masses of people and tons of produce were being transported. A day trip to Uxbridge, a market town, cost half a crown.

From Warwick Avenue underground walk down Clifton Villas, turning left into Blomfield Road. Moored in the Little Venice basin

Grand Union Canal, Little Venice

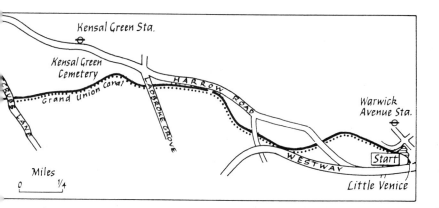

are several narrow boats, including one art gallery. Walk towards Westbourne Terrace Bridge from where you can look west along the route of the walk. Painted barges are moored on either side of the canal. The Canal Office is just below the bridge. On the right is a row of early Victorian houses and beside the canal a garden with giant classical columns and heraldic beasts belonging to Clifton Nurseries garden centre.

Join the towpath at the end of the Canal Office and walk past the moorings through the modern estates. As the canal curves south it meets the A40 as it curves above it. Even as the motorway carves through North Kensington, its silhouette creates an almost beautiful geometry. The tall chimney beside the canal on the left is part of Meanwhile Gardens, where local residents salvaged a piece of derelict land forgotten by the developers and made a children's playground.

After this you walk past the original and imposing Victorian waterways engineering – bridges, disused locks, and brick warehouses which back on to the river. The large white building on the right is Kensal House, owned by Virgin Records. By the bridge is The Narrow Boat pub.

After the bridge you might think you had reached the country. A bank of willows hides Kensal Green All Souls' Cemetery. As the path climbs up over a tributary, you can look over the trees at the classical Victorian memorials and temple. All Souls' was consecrated in 1833 as part of the Victorian attempt to ease overcrowding in London's cemeteries (page 100). Watergates in the southern wall allowed coffins to arrive by canal. Thackeray, Trollope, Leigh Hunt,

Charles Blondin and Princess Sophia, daughter of George III, are all buried here. In summer wildflowers flourish at the water's edge, even a rare, for London, clump of yellow flag.

Passing below two giant gasometers, surrounded by a hedge of blackberry, the towpath follows a bleak course along the south western railway line. Looking east you can see the Post Office Tower and the television transmitter at Crystal Palace.

In the shadow of the railway bridge, buddleia burst out of the cracks in the brick and in the train yard wildflowers have rooted themselves in the unhospitable soil.

Soon you reach Scrubs Lane and Wormwood Scrubs, the largest patch of greenery in the area. These 191 acres are dominated by the prison, the West London Stadium, and playing fields. Until the 1960s the Scrubs was used as a military training ground and the stadium stands on the site of the wartime arms depot. The prison was the last to be built in London. The work was carried out by prisoners, behind high walls, from 1874–90.

9 The Wandle

Length: almost 4 miles there and back. Rough going for pushchairs and too narrow in places for wheelchairs. Food: pub in Morden Road. Bus: No. 127. British Rail: Mitcham Junction one mile.

The Wandle rises near Croydon and flows eleven miles through Beddington, Merton and Tooting to join the Thames west of Wandsworth Bridge. In Merton the river is relatively clean and free-flowing, although the banks are concrete. In Wandsworth it sinks below a barrage of buildings and reaches the Thames through wasteland.

Mitcham Common, a large-sized patch of rough heathland, sprigged with gorse and thick with tangled woodland, is a good place

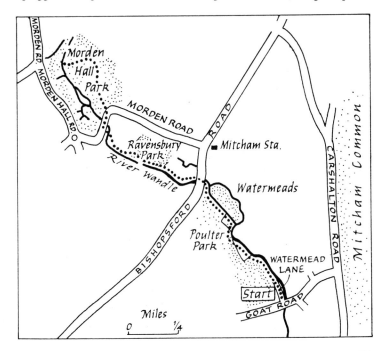

North of Watermead Lane

to walk, especially with dogs. It is rather like Wimbledon Common, though more cut up by roads. You could start walking from the Common, although this walk starts in Watermead Lane, where a terrace of small cottages overlooks the Wandle.

Beyond the cottages, the sides of the narrow footpath are overgrown in summer with high grass, nettles and cow parsley. The shallow Wandle sweeps over bright green weeds. There are elder, sycamore and hawthorn on the left, behind which are the Poulter Park playing fields. On the opposite bank is a small factory.

As the river bends round, the riverlands widen and several fallen trees block the path, but alternative routes have already been trodden. Two abandoned cars put one off walking here alone.

The path comes to an end at a fence behind which is Watermeads nature reserve, twelve acres of National Trust woodland. The undergrowth is thick with brambles and bluebells in spring and the woodlands are used to cultivate willows. The gates are locked, however, and you have to pay an annual subscription for a set of keys.

Take care of busy traffic crossing Bishopsford Road. The path now runs along the right-hand side of the river through Ravensbury estate. These modern flats have a marvellous view of the Wandle which has been landscaped to flow under wooden bridges past neat lawns. In spite of a fine oily film floating on the surface of the water, coots and ducks nest here.

In the middle of the eighteenth century there were two snuff mills at Ravensbury Bridge and two more at Morden Hall. The Wandle drove the waterwheels which ground the tobacco leaves into a powder. The Ravensbury mills turned to tobacco production at the beginning of the twentieth century and became famous for Mitcham Shag.

Cross Morden Road and turn right. Just before the pub a wooden door leads into Morden Hall Park. Follow the path through the avenue of chestnuts crossing channels of the Wandle, left from the milling days. Morden Hall was built in the seventeenth century and substantially rebuilt in 1840. Snuff continued to be produced at the Morden mills until the First World War when the hall was converted into a convalescent home for wounded soldiers. The estate was given to the National Trust in 1940. The hall is used as offices by Merton Borough Council and the lush parkland, where cattle, sheep and deer used to wander, is lined with horse chestnut trees. Having wandered round the park follow the river back to where you started, at the bottom of Watermead Lane.

10 Wapping and Rotherhithe

Length: about 3 miles. Fine for wheel- and pushchairs. Food: The Town of Ramsgate, The Mayflower, The Angel. To visit the River Police Museum ring 01–488–5399 first to make an appointment with the Administra-tive Inspector. Rotherhithe Heritage Museum: open weekdays from 10 a.m.–4 p.m. Ring first to make an appointment tel. 01–231–2976. Buses: Nos 15, 42, 47A, 56, 73. Undergound: Tower Hill.

From Tower Hill underground station follow signs to the Royal Mint and St Katharine's Dock from the subway to emerge by remains of the Roman and medieval city wall near St Katharine's Dock. Towering above a small water garden is the World Trade Centre, a vast brick and glass building just east of Tower Bridge. Cross the two bridges in the gardens and turn left over a wooden bridge to reach the dock.

It is a tremendous sight to see the tall masts of the sailing barges, tan sails furled, waving in the river breeze. St Katharine's may be a highly successful tourist attraction and it still smells of the seas. The dock was built in 1828 on the 25-acre site of the tenth-century hospital of St Katharine. The warehouses were used to stock wine, wool, spices, silver and ivory. It was heavily bombed during the Second World War and left derelict until development in 1968.

Walking clockwise round the dock you come to Ivory House, an Italianate building of 1854 which now houses a variety of shops. Passing under Ivory House and turning right past the Yacht Haven Office over a bridge you reach a round glass building, the Coronarium. Bear left under the Tower Hotel to reach the riverside and a large sundial (1973). Turn left here, cross the bridge and walk anticlockwise around Marble Quay. In the top left-hand corner is moored the *Nore*, a floating lightship used on the Thames estuary until 1943. To the right of the cobblestones stands the black weatherboarded Dickens Inn, built in the late 1700s as a brewery. It has been recently restored and is now a restaurant.

Walking round the back of a row of mock medieval brick houses

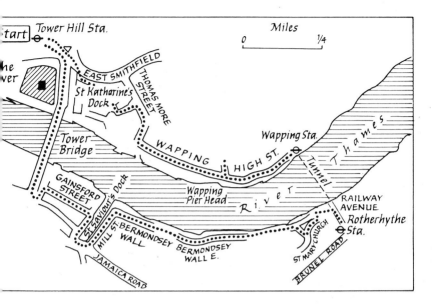

you reach the More Street car park. Walk out of the car park and turn right down Thomas More Street and left at the end of St Katharine's Way into Wapping High Street.

Wapping was marshland until drained in the early sixteenth century and protected by an earthen wall, with houses and shops on top. At Lower Wapping the dwellings had to be built on causeways. Shipbuilding and sea trade in the sixteenth and seventeenth centuries increased the population and brought in a bevy of seamen and pirates. In 1750 Wapping High Street had thirty-six taverns to keep them all happy.

At the top of the drainpipe of No. 11 Wapping High Street, by Wapping Old Stairs East, the date 1811 is engraved. The Old Stairs are reached through an alley, narrower than two arms' width, and at high tide the water thumps the steps, dousing two sturdy snapdragon plants. It was here that Captain Blood was caught red-handed trying to escape the City with the Crown Jewels.

The Town of Ramsgate at the corner of Old Stairs has been here since the seventeenth century. It used to be called the Red Cow, the place where the infamous Judge Jeffreys was captured whilst trying to escape to France. The Ramsgate is a narrow building with a small riverside garden where petty criminals were hung. Pirates were left tied to a post on the foreshore until drowned by the high tide. After

41

The City skyline from Bermondsey Wall

three days their swollen bodies so they say locally, originated the phrase 'what a wapper'.

Opposite The Town of Ramsgate is Scandrett Street. A few yards down on the right, opposite the church gardens, is St John of Wapping's charity school founded in 1695 and erected here by voluntary subscription in 1760. This moody building, now roofless and filled with buddleia, still has its boys' and infants' entrances decorated with pretty stone swags. Locally known as Scraps School it was closed during the Second World War. Next to it is the elegant brick clocktower of the Parish Church of St John, built in 1755–60 and bombed in 1940.

Return to the High Street, where Oliver's Wharf, a Victorian Gothic multi-coloured brick warehouse, was one of the first to be developed into luxury flats. Wapping New Stairs lead to a view across the river to St Mary's Church and The Angel in Rotherhithe (see below). On this side of the river is the River Police Pier.

The Thames River Police, founded in 1787, was the first police force of its kind. Formed to try to deal with escalating river theft, it never controlled the situation. Instead wet docks, completely surrounded by warehouses, and so more easily guarded, were built in 1805. The modern headquarters police headquarters of blue and cream glass and reinforced plastic is unbelievably hideous but contains an interesting museum.

King Henry's Stairs lead to a private jetty which, if open, offers a view of the back of King Henry's Wharf, one of the few still undeveloped. Walking along the High Street past further converted warehouses you reach Wapping underground station. If you have young children this would probably be a good place to end the walk.

If you are continuing, take the underground under the Thames to Rotherhithe. Before doing so you could take a detour to The Prospect of Whitby (No. 57 Wapping Wall), Wapping's other famous pub and, built *c*.1520, thought to be the oldest in London.

The Thames tunnel was originally designed by Marc Brunel for pedestrians. The first shaft was sunk in Rotherhithe in 1827. Building was supervised by Marc's son Isambard who celebrated his twenty-first birthday in the tunnel. After seven years' delay for want of funds, it finally reached its destination at Wapping in 1843. At first it was a popular method of crossing the river. Gradually it fell into disrepute and became a gathering point for thieves, drunks and whores and was sold to the London Railway Company in 1865.

Emerging in Brunel Road turn left immediately into Railway Avenue, a Victorian terrace of small brick cottages opposite Marc Brunel's Pumping House for the Thames Tunnel. Ahead lies Rope Knots Garden, a small paved riverside garden with giant Borrower-like nautical knots made of iron recalling the local rope-making trade. Turning left into Rotherhithe Street, which is narrow and dark, you reach The Mayflower, from which Captain Christopher Jones, a local man, sailed the *Mayflower* in 1620 to explore the New World. The original inn was built in about 1550, rebuilt in the eighteenth century and recently restored.

Turn left down St Marychurch Street to the entrance to St Mary's Church, built between 1715 and 1737. It is a beautiful church of red brick with white stone quoins. The tower was added in 1747 and the spire in 1861. The piers are made of ships' masts. The altar in the Lady's Chamber and the two bishops' chairs are built from timber from the *Téméraire* which was brought to rest in Rotherhithe. Turner painted *The Fighting Téméraire* in Rotherhithe.

Outside the church gates stands St Mary Rotherhithe Free School founded in 1613 and established here in 1797 in this three-storey, three-bay house built in about 1700. The charity boy and girl still stand in niches above the front door. Before leaving the school look at the small brick building, St Mary's Watchhouse, built in 1821. Returning to Rotherhithe Street turn left and walk between the warehouses past the Rotherhithe Heritage Museum which contains treasures from the Thames foreshore.

Keep following the river along Rotherhithe Street to Fulford Street. Cut across the grass to Cathay Street and King's Stairs Gardens, which contain a map of the skyline showing St Paul's, the Monument, the National Westminster Tower and the Lloyd's building. At the other end of the garden, overlooking the river, stands the white weatherboarded pub The Angel, which dates back to the sixteenth century. In the square patch of derelict land southeast of Cathay Street excavations are being carried out (at the time of writing) of the Palace of Edward III.

From The Angel walk along Bermondsey Wall East, named after Bermondsey Abbey, founded here in 1089. Bermondsey Wall East continues past a large piece of derelict land offering constantly changing views of the riverside. Bermondsey Wall West brings you to the frenzy of building work that is changing Bermondsey. The warehouses and mills that stored and ground spices, grain and flours are being converted into blocks of flats. Roads may be blocked to allow works machinery through so be prepared to alter your route.

At the top of Mill Street stands New Concordia Wharf. Originally part of St Saviour's Flour Mill, it was converted in 1981–3 and provides an example of how this area will look when completely redeveloped. Walking down Mill Street you pass Jacob Street, site of the notorious Victorian slum Jacob's Island and where Dickens killed off Bill Sykes in *Oliver Twist*. In the next street down, Wolseley Street, you can see the disused Victorian factory buildings of Jacob's Biscuits with separate 'Office' and 'Workers' entrances.

Walking round St Saviour's Dock, once used by the monks of Bermondsey Abbey, you reach Shad Thames, a corruption of St John at Thames, from the days when the Knights of the Order of St John owned the land around here. If the top end of Shad Thames is still closed off for the development of Butler's Wharf, Gainsford Street leads just as well to Horsleydown Lane where you will find The Anchor Tap, the first pub John Courage established, and which now sells Samuel Smith's ale. From here turn right into Elizabeth Street and right again to cross Tower Bridge.

RURAL WALKS

11 Chiswick House Gardens

Length: about 1 mile. Fine for push- and wheelchairs. Food: café in Chiswick Gardens. The house is open daily, except on Mondays and Tuesdays in winter. Tel. 01–994–3299. Buses: Nos 290, E3. Underground: Turnham Green is about ten minutes' walk away.

Only yards from the Great West Road, a high brick wall keeps the secret of Chiswick House and gardens. From the main gates in Burlington Lane a magnificent tree-lined avenue leads to Lord Burlington's fabulous Palladian villa, built in 1725–9 as a showcase for his art collection and somewhere to entertain friends. Double staircases lead to a two-storey portico, flanked with statues of

An avenue north of the villa

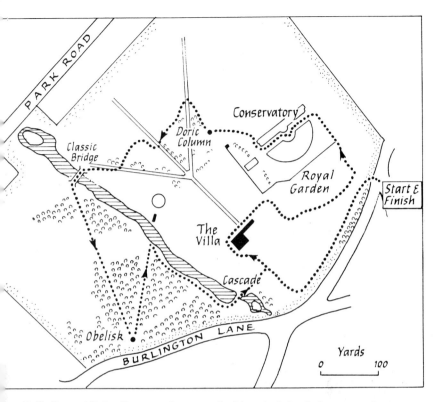

Palladio and Inigo Jones and crowned with a dark leaded octagonal dome. Lord Burlington, the greatest patron of the arts of his day, started a new fashion in England by modelling his villa on the sixteenth-century Italian architect Palladio's Villa Capra near Vicenza.

The gardens, designed by William Kent, were as innovative as the villa. Instead of planting a geometric garden as had been the tradition throughout the seventeenth century, he introduced a more natural, romantic style.

Walk anticlockwise around the house, past the avenue, to the large stone gateway built by Inigo Jones and turn right along the hedged path past the Royal Gardens to the Conservatory in the Italian Gardens. Around Joseph Paxton's conservatory, an ancient, gnarled wistaria winds, serpent-like, and under the glass panes grow tall camellias. On the lawns outside are described two 'S'-shapes of hyacinth and forget-me-not.

A narrow gravelled track leads from the far end of the conservatory to a Doric column and north along an avenue of young beech to a cobbled path hidden by yews. Turn left along this avenue to reach the focal point of three radiating avenues. Originally there was a folly at the end of each avenue. Follow the central avenue and turn left through a gap in the hedge to walk through the wilderness, a romantic tangle of woodland and wildflowers.

Keep bearing left through the wood until you reach the western avenue. To the left stands an Ionic temple overlooking a round pond in the centre of which stands an obelisk. Turn right to reach James Wyatt's high-arched, ornamental Classic Bridge which replaced the original wooden footbridge in 1788. Cross the bridge and walk down the avenue through the woods to another obelisk. Take the next avenue back towards the Long Water and follow the western bank to its end in a cascade of water over rough-hewn rock, and then follow the path back to the main drive.

12 Dulwich to Sydenham Hill Wood

Length: 4 miles round trip. Push- and wheelchairs can be taken to the end of Cox's Walk, but not into the woods. Food: pubs in Dulwich, café in Dulwich Park. Note: Sydenham Hill Wood is a nature reserve and you should therefore stick to the paths. Buses: Nos 3, 37, 68. British Rail: North Dulwich, Herne Hill.

Dulwich was a sleepy rural village of less than 2,000 people until the discovery in the 1850s of a spa. Dulwich Wells, which stood at the corner of Lordship Lane and Dulwich Common, brought the crowds and with them business and expansion. By 1901 Dulwich contained over 10,000 people. Yet much of the old meadows and woods of the medieval manor of Dulwich have survived and Dulwich Village, as the old high street is called, still looks like a village street.

Walk south along Dulwich Village past the burial ground where Old Bridget, the Queen of the Gypsies, was buried in 1768. The wide street is lined with Victorian cottages, few cars and wide grass verges –

Bell Cottage

49

all that remains of the common lands, known locally as the Manor Wastes. At the end of the shops begins a row of Georgian villas.

Through the wrought-iron gates behind the roundabout you can see Dulwich Old College, founded by the celebrated Shakespearian actor, Edward Alleyn who was also Master Overseer and Ruler of the Bears, Bulls and Mastiff Dogs at the Bear Gardens, Bankside (page 142). Alleyn bought the Manor of Dulwich for £5,000 in 1616. Being childless, he decided to build a charitable school which he called the Chapel and College of God's Gift. At the roundabout, bear left past Woodyard Lane, turning left into Dulwich Park through the main gates opposite Dulwich Picture Gallery.

Dulwich Park was opened in 1890 by Lord Rosebery, first Chairman of the London County Council. Like Battersea Park, Dulwich has a municipal air about its planned boating lake, tea house, rhododendrons and shrubberies. For all that, it stands on the old meadows and, as you walk clockwise around the park's perimeter road, there is a stretch of open land between the park and the houses.

Leaving the park by Rosebery Gate, turn left and walk along Dulwich Common road. Opposite The Harvester, through a kissing gate, is Cox's Walk, a tarmac track leading through oaks to Sydenham Hill Wood. The path ends beside a footbridge over disused Crystal Palace railway lines from where Pissarro painted a view of Lordship Lane. Cross the bridge and walk up the logged steps to the right. The wood is dark and surprisingly small for the great variety of wildlife it supports. Once part of the Great North Wood, established after the Ice Age, Sydenham contains 138 species of plants and 52 types of tree. Oaks and hornbeam form a high canopy over a good variety of bush and shrub.

In the centre of the wood the only signs of the railway line, which was closed in 1954, are the overgrown embankments, the footbridge and a boarded-up tunnel. Especially after rain, the wood smells wonderful and standing still you hear all the birds. Fifty-three species have been counted here.

Following the numbered posts backwards, beside post number four you will find the remains of a Gothic folly. Climb up a gravel path, laid down by volunteers from the London Wildlife Trust, who manage the woods, to reach a clearing at post three.

The ornamental trees in this area were planted in the gardens of Victorian houses on the south-eastern edge of the wood which were demolished in the 1960s. Through a natural arch in the trees, down

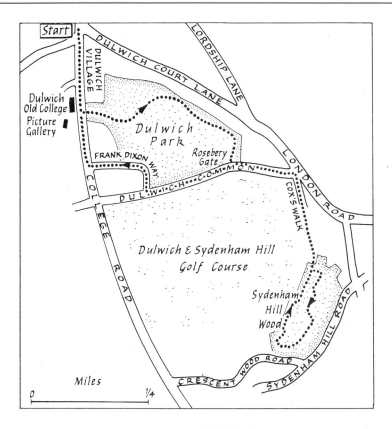

Start

LORDSHIP LANE

DULWICH VILLAGE

DULWICH COURT LANE

Dulwich Old College

Picture Gallery

Dulwich Park

FRANK DIXON WAY

Rosebery Gate

LONDON ROAD

D U L W I C H C O M M O N

COLLEGE ROAD

Dulwich & Sydenham Hill Golf Course

COX'S WALK

Sydenham Hill Wood

SYDENHAM HILL ROAD

CRESCENT WOOD ROAD

Miles

0   ¼

some wooden steps, is the London Wildlife Trust hut beside the old train tunnel. Turn right here and right again, following the gravel path past a small pond dug in 1984, surrounded by marsh plants.

At post six, turn left and follow the wire fence to Cox's Walk and walk back along Dulwich Common. Turn down Frank Dixon Way which brings you out on College Road, by the 1767 brick Bell House behind high chestnut trees and next to Bell Cottage, weather-boarded with grey-blue shutters.

Further down on your left is Dulwich Picture Gallery, the first public art gallery in England. It dates back to 1626 when Edward Alleyn bequeathed his collection of thirty-nine paintings. This was substantially increased in 1811 and the gallery built to house it. Designed by John Soane and built of stock brick, it was completed in 1814.

13 Greenwich and Blackheath

Length: 3 miles there and back. Suitable for push- and wheelchairs. Food: pubs and restaurants in Greenwich and Tranquil Vale. The river boat to Greenwich Pier leaves hourly from Westminster, Charing Cross and Tower Piers. Buses: Nos 56, 277 to the Isle of Dogs; 1, 180, 185, 188, 286 to Greenwich. British Rail: Greenwich, Blackheath. Light Railway: Island Gardens.

From Island Gardens the view across the river to Greenwich Palace is the one Christopher Wren, its designer, liked best. In the corner of the gardens crouches a strange glass dome, the entrance to the underwater Thames Passenger Footpath, built in 1902, from which you will emerge at an identical dome in the shadow of the *Cutty Sark* at Greenwich.

This vast Victorian tea and wool clipper, with its heavy timbers and complicated rigging, supporting three-quarters of an acre of canvas, towers above Francis Chichester's *Gypsy Moth IV*. Having voyaged around the world in 1967 the *Gypsy Moth* now rests here, dwarfed even by the rusty barges moored off shore.

The town of Greenwich is packed with antique and book shops, old houses and pubs. Greenwich Market, granted its charter by William III in 1700, has been on this site since 1737. Having looked around, start the walk by heading along King William Walk past the entrance to The Queen's House and the National Maritime Museum, the first Palladian villa in England, built by Inigo Jones and a building of endless beauty. Wren added the domed painted hall and the chapel, redecorated after a fire in 1779.

Such seventeenth- and eighteenth-century perfections make it seem as though Greenwich had no other history. But Bronze Age burial grounds and a Roman villa belonging to a small fishing village have been found. The first manor was built in 1427 by the Duke of Gloucester, Henry V's brother. Henry VI made it a royal residence, but it was Henry VIII who loved hunting deer here and used it most.

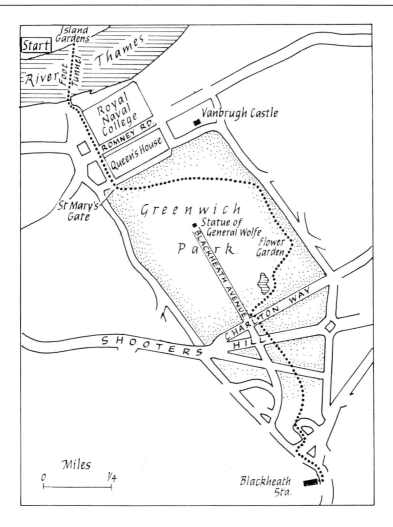

Greenwich Park was enclosed in 1433 by Henry VI's uncle, the powerful Duke of Gloucester, but the formal landscaping and great avenues of chestnuts that distinguish it still were designed for Charles II by Le Nôtre. My favourite spot in the park is the steep round hill, crowned with dark thorn trees, that you see ahead immediately you enter St Mary's Gate. At the top of the hill there's a magnificent view from 155 feet up, back across the Thames. Between the black steeples, tower blocks and cranes are the

The Royal Observatory

silhouettes of the Post Office Tower and St Paul's. Then the river loops north again, its grey skin burnished by the sun.

At the beginning of the seventeenth century, John Vanbrugh built himself a castle, which you can see beyond the eastern park walls; he lived here whilst surveying the construction of Greenwich Hospital.

From the top of the hill avenues of wrinkled sweet chestnut lead to the Flower Garden, formally arranged with summer beds of incandescent tulips and scented hyacinth amongst vast cedars and a seventeenth-century sweet chestnut notched with lovers' initials.

Keeping to the perimeter of the flower garden you pass the Wilderness, thirteen acres of woodland behind a high wire fence. A herd of fallow deer lives here and some rare birds: the spotted flycatcher, whitethroat, bullfinch, willow warbler and coal tit.

Head towards the ornamental lake and keeping it to your right you come to Blackheath Avenue. Turn left here and walk out of Greenwich Park on to the heath. Blackheath gets its name from its dark soil, once crowded with the roots of trees and shrubs. These made the heath popular with highwaymen who sometimes ended up swinging from the tall gibbet on Shooters Hill. Wat Tyler massed his peasant army here in 1381, Henry V was welcomed back victorious from Agincourt in 1415 and the crowds gathered again to see Charles II's Restoration Army.

Until the Second World War the heath was rough with gravel pits and wildlife. Army equipment was stored here during the war and afterwards the gravel pits were filled in and the heath became the bold flat green it is today. Below a darkening sky, Blackheath can seem quite menacing. On a summer day, the majestic eighteenth- and nineteenth-century villas put up with donkey rides, kites, picnics and bikinis. Tranquil Vale, a steep, terraced shopping street, runs downhill from the south-west corner of the heath. It is an unusual and lovely wide street with narrow cobbled alleys slipped in between the shops and houses.

Either end the walk here and return home from Blackheath Station or go back to Greenwich Park. At the main park gates Blackheath Avenue leads to the Royal Observatory, built in 1675 for John Flamsteed, the first Astronomer Royal. On the way to it you pass the tea house and an ornate scarlet and black bandstand. At the top of the avenue are the Planetarium, Observatory and the Meridian Line. From here it's an easy walk down the hill to St Mary's Gate.

14 The Hadley Wood Giant

Length: between ½ and 2 miles. Not suitable for push- or wheelchairs. Food: take a picnic. Buses:	Nos 84, 263. Underground: High Barnet.

Monken Hadley Common is mostly wooded, the remains of the royal forest of Enfield Chase. Coming from Hadley take Hadley Green Road and turn left after the church down Camlet Way. The walk proper begins opposite the convent school.

Walk east across open heathland towards the woods, which were enclosed in 1777. There are routes through the woods, though no marked paths. The ground can be marshy and it is a good idea to take

Jake finds the Giant

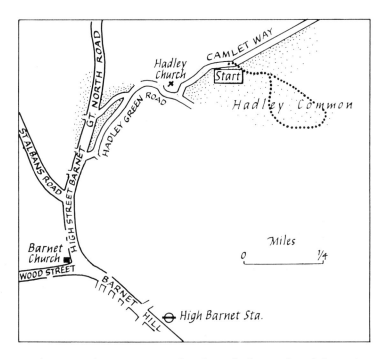

gumboots so that you can trudge through the mud and deceptive bogs – not that they are dangerous, just wet. The canopy is mainly oak, hornbeam, beech and ash; holly and bramble, including dog roses, flourish in the dappled shade. There are ferns, heath rushes, sedges and a variety of common wildflowers like rosebay willowherb and the small yellow silverweed.

The aim of this walk is to find the sleeping giant. The wooden giant has slept for so long that his great body, perhaps twenty feet of twigs and branches twisted into the sinews of a man, has become a part of the forest. The giant was actually constructed by untrained artist Ben Wilson only a few years ago.

The directions are simple enough. Enter the tall wood, walk east for about half a mile, cross two small plank bridges and there he is. The trouble is that, like Pan, the giant plays tricks and you can spend an hour wandering through the woods before you find him.

15 Hampstead Heath

Length: 3 miles round trip. Rough going in parts for push- and wheelchairs. Food: café at Kenwood. Kenwood House woodlands are open from 8 a.m. to dusk. The house is open daily; for details tel. 01–348–1286. Buses: Nos 53, 214, C11. Underground: Tufnell Park. British Rail: Gospel Oak.

Extending over more than eight hundred acres of north London, Hampstead Heath attracts sometimes as many as a hundred thousand people a day. This walk keeps to the wilder side of the heath, away from the popular Jack Straw's Castle pub on the western edge. There are paths, but it's more fun if you don't need to use them.

The best time to walk is early in the morning when the mist still curls around the crest of the hills and hides the church spires of Highgate. Starting from the entrance opposite Swain's Lane in Highgate Road, follow Nightingale Lane along the lower contours of Parliament Hill, by Highgate Ponds. The six ponds are very different in character. The first is quite formal and surrounded by willows trailing their fragile branches. The second is for men to swim in. The third is for sailing model boats. The fourth, fenced off as a wildlife sanctuary, is by far the most attractive. The pond water laps the reedy shore, and marsh marigolds and cuckoo flowers grow in the bog. Fallen trees are left to rot on the damp soil, turning a brilliant green as they become covered in moss. The fifth pond is the Ladies' Pond and the sixth the Stock Pond.

Parliament Hill rises on your left, a smooth green mound sliced by ancient hawthorn hedges, now so overgrown that they stand as individual trees. Follow the path after the boating pond left round the edge of Parliament Hill. If you don't have a pushchair you can turn off the path to the right and climb the gentle slope through rough grass and small copses. If you need to stick to the path continue until you reach the crossing of the paths in the middle of the heath and take the first path to the right which leads up the hill towards Kenwood House. Until the thirteenth century wolves

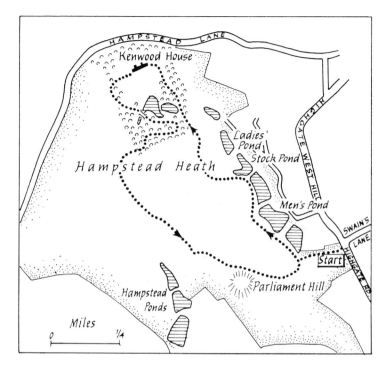

roamed these hills and in Henry VIII's day washerwomen gathered here to scrub the filth from the clothes of London's nobility.

Today there are over eighty different bird species on the heath and the plant life, first recorded in the sixteenth century in Gerard's *Herbal*, is rich. When you reach the entrance to the Woodland Garden, where children and dogs have to be kept under control, follow the path all the way to Kenwood House. These woodlands are thought to be part of the ancient Forest of Middlesex and have been designated a Site of Special Scientific Interest. The path through the wood is ribbed with hard roots and fenced off from the trees which grow thickly on either side.

You emerge from the woods by the Concert Pond (where concerts are given during the summer) at the bottom of a long grassy hill at the top of which stands Kenwood House. Underneath its eighteenth-century stucco façade (Robert Adam and George Saunders) stands the seventeenth-century brick house. Kenwood now contains the Iveagh Bequest, a collection of paintings bequeathed by Edward

Parliament Hill

Guinness, 1st Earl of Iveagh, in 1927, including works by Gains-borough, Van Dyck, Reynolds, Lawrence, Landseer, Guardi, Rembrandt and Turner. Walking behind the house through the small formal gardens you pass Dr Johnson's summerhouse.

Returning through the western edge of the woods to the crest of Parliament Hill and back to the start, there's a marvellous view of London spreading below.

16 Hampton Court and Bushy Park

Length: about 7½ miles. This walk is not suitable for push- and wheelchairs, though there are paths you can use instead. Food: restaurants and pubs in Hampton Court Road, the café at Hampton Court. Hampton Court Palace Park and Gardens are open daily from 9 a.m. to dusk or 9 p.m. and from 2 p.m. on Sundays. Hampton Court Palace is open daily except New Year, Christmas and Easter. For details tel. 01–977–8441. Buses: Nos 111, 131, 216, 267, 461, 715, 716, 718, 726. British Rail: Hampton Court.

Between them Hampton Court Park and Bushy Park cover nearly 1,700 acres of land caught in a wide crook of the Thames. Hampton means 'the farm in the bend of the river' in Anglo-Saxon. The dry and acid soil produces rough, tussocky heathland, of a better quality at Hampton, which is nearer the river.

Hampton belonged to the Knights Hospitaller of St John of Jerusalem until 1514 when Thomas Wolsey bought it, a year before becoming Cardinal and Lord Chancellor of England. He knocked down the old manor, enclosed both parks and built himself a wonderful palace which he offered to King Henry VIII in 1526 in a vain attempt to win back his sovereign's favour. It didn't work, and in 1529 Henry seized the Cardinal's goods and lands and was soon making major changes to Hampton Court.

Oliver Cromwell, incidentally, put Hampton up for sale; the proceeds were to go to the Commonwealth, but in 1651 he thought better of it and moved in himself with his family.

From the Lion Gates in Hampton Court Road, walk through the Wilderness – wilder now than it was when William and Mary arranged clipped yews like a richly embroidered fabric. This leads to the east front of the palace, rebuilt by Wren for William III. These seventeenth-century Renaissance balustrades and pediments seem to me a poor companion to the fantastic detail, intricacy and romance of the Tudor palace.

Three avenues of yew step in a *patte d'oie* (goose-foot shape)

61

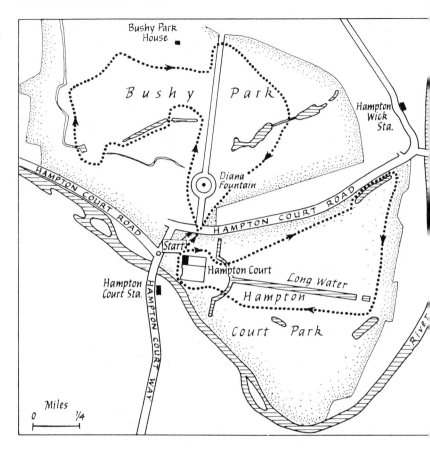

across the Long Water, becoming avenues of vast limes in Hampton Court Park. When planted for Charles II, the yews were sheared into elegant obelisks. Over the years they have bulged into squat green pyramids. Follow the left-hand avenue, across the water through the wrought-iron gate into the parkland. The ancient limes were torn out, in the 1987 storms, leaving raw craters in the red soil around which herds of red and fallow deer and sheep pasture. The parkland, once fringed with trees, is now edged by tower blocks.

Even before winter is out, the first lambs have been born and the young tips of the willows around Hampton Wick Pond tinge the sad branches yellow-green. Later in the year the bullrushes shoot up. The twelve-sided red-brick ice house was built in 1626 by Charles II who had brought the secret of refrigeration with him from France.

From the head of the Long Water the avenue leads back to the palace. Walking into the picture and towards the palace you follow the Long Water back through the southern gate to the palace gardens.

To the south is the Elizabethan Knot Garden, leading to the river and the Privy Garden, planted with tall shrubs hiding classical statues, which leads towards twelve beautiful wrought-iron screens overlooking the river. These were made by Jean Tijou, a seventeenth-century ironworker. Close by you will find the Great Vine: planted by Capability Brown in 1768, its grapes are sold to the public in late August/September.

Walk back through the gardens to the Lion Gates and across Hampton Court Road to the main entrance to Bushy Park, given to the public by Queen Victoria in 1838. It is rather like Richmond Park on a smaller scale, having the same tough yellow heath grass. Charles I and Oliver Cromwell both tried, and failed, to claim it for themselves. Charles I had a tributary of the Colne River diverted through Bushy Park, making the Longford River which flows to the Long Water at Hampton Court and into the Thames. He also commissioned what is called the Diana Fountain from Francesco Fanelli, although actually the bronze statue is of Arethusa, the wood nymph whom Diana changed into a stream to save her from the love of the river god Alpheus. Cromwell made the Heron and Leg-of-Mutton ponds at the east end of the park.

The mile-long Chestnut Avenue of 274 trees planted 42 feet apart was designed by Christopher Wren for William III. Every year, on Chestnut Sunday (the Sunday nearest 11 May) Londoners came to Bushy to see the chestnut blossom. Walk along the avenue bearing left after the Diana Fountain, to enter the Woodland Gardens, planted in 1949.

Within the wooden fence the river meanders along green mossy banks, through carpets of flowers and every kind of shrub and tree. Kingfishers, woodpeckers, tree creepers and nuthatches are a few of the eighty birds that visit Bushy Park. Kestrel, tawny owl and little owl are some of the rarer nesting birds. Follow the stream west, crossing the wooden bridge and continue along the path to cross back over the stream at the second bridge. Follow the stream to the gatekeeper's cottage and a gate. Leave by the gate, cross the path and go through the gate opposite into the second woodland garden.

Continue alongside the stream, keeping the boundary of the

Hampton Court from the east end of the Long Water

garden on your right. Turn right at the gate at the north-eastern edge of the garden and right again along the road, passing a car park on your right. On your left is Bushy Park House, a fine red-brick Georgian building lived in by William IV when he was the Duke of Clarence.

Cross Chestnut Avenue, and bear south-east over the grass, past a drinking fountain towards a group of oaks. Bear right through the trees to reach a road which you cross, making your way to Leg-of-Mutton Pond. Cross the bridge to walk south, past the Diana Fountain and out of the main gates.

17 Holland Park

Length: 2 miles round trip. Fine
for push- and wheelchairs. Linley
Sambourne's house: tel. 01–994–
1079 for opening times. Food:
café in Holland Park, the Elephant
and Castle, Holland Street. Buses:
Nos 18, 22, 290. Underground:
Holland Park, Kensington High
Street.

Although Holland Park is one of the loveliest central London parks,
it doesn't take very long to walk around, so this walk continues to
thread through the Georgian and Victorian alleys and streets west of
the park.

From Holland Park underground station, cross the road and turn

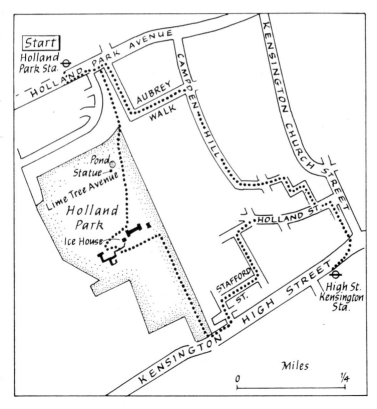

65

left to reach the road called Holland Park and turn right up it, walking on the left-hand side below a white stone wall. Turn left at the end of the wall through an arch into the park.

Holland Park stands on part of the old Manor of Abbots Kensington which was bought by Walter Cope, James I's Chancellor of the Exchequer, who owned nearly all of Kensington. Cope began building a house, Cope's Castle, which became known as Holland House after his death when his son-in-law, the Earl of Holland took it over. Holland lost his head during the Civil War and Cromwell's General Fairfax quickly moved in.

After the Restoration the estate was returned to the Holland family. Joseph Addison married the widow of the 3rd Earl Holland and probably composed his *Spectator* essays pacing up and down the Long Gallery, glass in hand.

Walk up the hill through the Wilderness, fifty-five acres of mixed oak, elm, birch, plane and sycamore, the largest natural woodland in central London. Disorderliness is its charm. Much of the woodland, overgrown with briars and brambles, is fenced off, but you can wander along the rough tracks down to the pond and the statue of the 3rd Earl Holland, by G. F. Watts and J. E. Boehm. In the clearing ahead bluebells, daffodils and crocuses flower in spring. Some fallen trees are deliberately left to rot to attract a greater variety of wildlife.

Turning left just before the Lime Tree avenue, follow the path through woods to the North Lawn. On the other side of this are remains of the original seventeenth-century walls of Holland House, where men like Byron, Sydney Smith, Earl Grey, Wordsworth, Scott, Palmerston, Sheridan, Dickens and Macaulay met. Bomb damage in 1940 reduced the house to ruins in which state it remained until it was sold to the London County Council in 1952. The original weathered red-brick wall is separated by a moat from the King George VI Memorial Youth Hostel, sympathetically designed by Hugh Casson and opened in 1959. The tower is a replica of one of two on the original house.

Turn right and follow the path to the end of Holland House. Turn left here, into the Dutch Garden, at its best in April, filled with scented polyanthus, hyacinths and wallflowers. Together with dark pansies, tall tulips and a cloud of blue forget-me-not they grow thickly in formal box-hedged beds. A peacock on the garden wall, the remains of the stables built in 1640, picks its way amongst the creepers and occasionally mews like a scared cat.

Chestnut Tree Avenue in Holland Park

At the end of the garden turn right and double back to the old ice house, now an art gallery. On your left is the best park café I know. Walk underneath the tiled brick walkway ahead, built in 1857–8 to link what was then the ballroom and is now the Orangery with the main house and head east and south, walking around the playing field to High Street, Kensington.

The walk now leaves the park by the main gates on to Kensington High Street. Turn left and then left again, up Phillimore Gardens. The Italianate houses in this estate were built between 1855 and 1874 by Charles Phillimore. In spring the streets are shaded by the blossom-heavy boughs of cherry trees. Turn right into Stafford Terrace. One of the first residents, the *Punch* cartoonist Linley Sambourne, lived at No. 18 which is now preserved as a museum. Turning left into Argyll Road you pass the end of Phillimore Place where Kenneth Grahame, author of *The Wind in the Willows*, lived at No. 16.

Turn right at the end of Upper Phillimore Gardens and cross Campden Hill Road into Holland Street passing the northern end of Kensington Town Hall. The eastern section of Holland Street is marked with a square blue-tiled road sign on the north cornerhouse. This is a lovely street of Georgian and Victorian houses, antique shops, art bookshops and restaurants.

Facing the pub a small cul-de-sac leads between the leafy front gardens of an early Victorian terrace. In summer pale pink roses tumble over the railings and, since there is no room for cars, it is as if you are looking into the last century.

Turn right down Kensington Church Walk along a narrow lane of shops leading to St Mary Abbots Church. Designed by George Gilbert Scott in the 1870s, it has the third highest spire of any parish church in England. The church gardens were converted from an old burial ground and you can still see the old red-brick mortuary at the far end of the gardens. Standing above the entrance to St Mary Abbots primary school are the brightly painted figures of a boy and girl which survive from the charity school designed by Nicholas Hawksmoor in 1705.

If you wanted you could end the walk here, close to Kensington High Street underground station. Otherwise walk back up the hill turning left into Holland Street and right up Gordon Place. Make a detour at the junction with Pitt Street to turn right and walk past the Carmelite Monastery in Duke's Lane. The monastery was built in 1886–9. Queen Anne's Cottages opposite are late eighteenth century and Gordon Cottages were built in around 1850.

Returning to Gordon Place turn left and right up Campden Hill Road where you pass Observatory Gardens. James South, astronomer and president of the Royal Astronomical Society, lived here in 1827–67 and built himself an observatory in his garden on top of the hill.

Continue up Campden Hill Road, a fairly steep hill and turn left into Aubrey Walk which leads to Aubrey House. This was built in the 1690s over a medicinal spring, said to 'take off the Acidity of the Juices and Blood, and to Incarnate and suit in Heartburns and some sort of Phthises and may agree with the Cold and Phlegmatick best.' From here it's a short walk down Holland Park Avenue the underground or bus.

18 Nunhead Cemetery to Peckham Rye

Length: 2 miles round trip. Push- and wheelchairs can be taken the whole way. Food: The Belvedere at the corner of Nunhead and Linden Groves. Bus: No. P3. British Rail: Nunhead.

From the main stone gates of Nunhead Cemetery in Linden Grove, the wide gravel drive leads to a deserted Gothic Anglican chapel. Clouds pass behind the windows in a frame of crumbling stone and

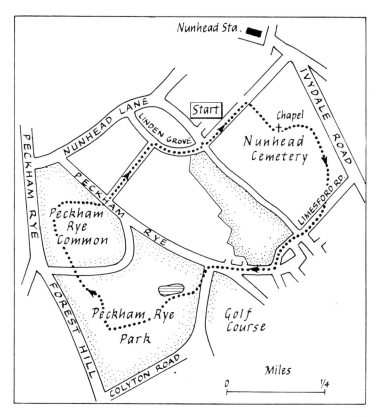

69

Nunhead Cemetery

dark green creeper. The arched entrance is boarded up and daubed with a red 'Danger' sign. On either side of the drive the overgrown grass verges are knee-high with timothy grass, buttercups and fat purple clover in summer.

When Nunhead Cemetery was consecrated in 1840 the clipped verges would have led through rows of tombstones and yews. A hundred years later the cemetery was abandoned. Vandals destroyed much, including the chapel, and the cemetery was closed in 1969. In 1975 Southwark Council took it over, began clearing it up and since 1980 Nunhead has been open for burials.

As you walk up the drive you realise that the tall dark woods on either side are thick with tombstones: twenty-foot-high granite columns, and stone obelisks tilting more outrageously than the tower of Pisa. But in the trees, many of them rapid-growing syacamore saplings, are tombs, graves and crosses draped with broad, dark ivy. Ivy grasps the tree trunks climbing thirty or forty feet high, one of the few plants that can survive under this dense canopy.

Walking clockwise around the cemetery, you pass signs of recent burials, especially on the approach to the gates on Limesford Road.

Leave the cemetery here, turn right, and continue into Borland Road. Turn right into Stuart Road, past terraces of Victorian cottages to reach the corner of Peckham Rye Park.

The entrance to the park is about twenty yards down Homestall Road where a path leads past a good wooden adventure playground to an ornamental lake. The park was opened in 1894 as an extension to Peckham Rye Common. Walking clockwise again round the park past the English Garden, cross Straker's Road on to the common, a rough-grass open space with some trees and a horseride.

At the northern edge of the common, follow Solomon's Passage to Forester Road and turn right into Linden Grove, where you started.

19 Osterley Park

Length: about 2 miles. Fine for wheel- or pushchairs except around the lake. Food: the cafeteria in the stable block is open from April to the end of October.

The grounds are open daily. The house is open every day except Monday. For details tel. 01–560–3918. Bus: No. 91. Underground: Osterley (ten-minute walk).

A hundred yards from the foul A4, Osterley Village sits with its local post office, branch bank, newsagent, farm and manor house, as if it were a village in the heart of Oxfordshire.

The entrance to Osterley Park is through gates at the end of the village with the house at the end of an avenue through fields. The land is farmed by Osterley Park Farm, part of which you pass on your right. You can buy cheap, freshly picked produce in season and visits round the farm can be arranged.

This is the description of Osterley in the sixteenth century:

> The house, . . . a faire and stately building of bricke, [was] erected by Sir Thomas Gresham, Knight, Citizen and Marchant-Adventurer of London, and finished about anno 1577. It standeth in a parke by him also impaled, well-wooded, and garnished with manie faire ponds, which afforde not only fish and fowle, as swanes, and other water fowle, but also great use for milles, as paper milles, oyle milles, and corne milles, all of which are now decayed.

Osterley has had a succession of illustrious owners. Thomas Gresham was founder of the Royal Exchange and his four-towered house is now encased in an eighteenth-century Palladian villa. Nicholas Barbon, who bought it in 1683, brought in the idea of fire insurance after the Great Fire of London. After his death the house was bought by Francis Child, who became an MP, Lord Mayor and a Knight. Child was the first goldsmith to start managing people's money and became known as the 'father of banking'. If you have never been inside, do look round. It is a showpiece of Adam design. The antechamber is one of the few rooms in the world that is exactly as it was in the eighteenth century – floor-to-ceiling rich, red Gobelin tapestry.

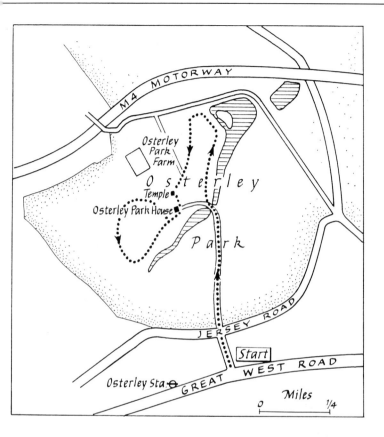

At the southern edge of the lake there is still a bird sanctuary
which you can't enter; over eighty species of bird have been recorded
at Osterley in one year, including the kingfisher. The many ponds
have become a long serpentine lake, designed by William Chambers
in the 1750s to appear as a natural tributary of the Thames.

Bear right off the avenue to walk round the lake which is so
established that it seems quite wild. When the Child family lived
here they sailed a Chinese sampan on the water and took tea in a
Chinese teahouse. The only echo of those days is the reconstructed
floating Chinese summerhouse, decorated in red, eau-de-Nil and
gold. When you reach the northern perimeter of the lake, the sight of
a thundering coach and roar of a plane taking off from Heathrow
remind you how close the city is.

Cross the flat, open parklands, with wonderful views of the house,

The Elizabethan stables

and head towards the Elizabethan stable blocks. During the week there are few visitors. Behind the stable block are the gardens, laid out by William Chambers in the eighteenth century as an Arcadian pleasure garden. Follow the gravel paths through planted beds of evergreen shrubs, past a Doric temple dedicated to Pan and originally used as a dining room. Almost opposite this is Robert Adam's semi-circular greenhouse, built in the 1770s and then used as an outdoor room. From here walk in a wide anti-clockwise loop through the woods returning past the north-western end of the lake to the main drive.

20 Eltham Common to Oxleas Wood

Length: about 5 miles round trip. Not suitable for wheel- or push-chairs. Food: take a picnic. Buses: Nos 89, 178, 402. If possible take a car and park in Red Lion Lane.

This walk could easily be extended via Sheperdleas Wood (south of Rochester Way) to Eltham Parks North and South, Avery Hill Park and thereby to Eltham High Street.

From the junction of Shooters Hill and Well Hall Road, take the first main track into the woods off the south side of Shooters Hill. This is just beyond the bus stop and marked with a signpost. Follow the left-hand track through the oak woods, up a slight incline to reach a tarmac path by some school playing fields. There is a large yellow sign here with a map of Oxleas Wood. Turn right along the path into Castle Wood and start following the wooden posts for the Green Chain Walk.

You soon reach Severndroog Castle, dedicated in 1784 to

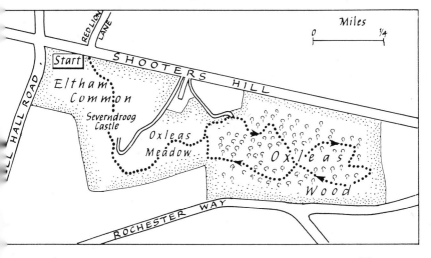

Remnants of a thorn hedge, Oxleas Meadow

William James of Eltham Park who conquered the Castle of Severndroog off the coast of Malabar. The grey three-cornered crenellated fortress, boarded up and scrawled on, is a depressing sight.

Continuing down some steps to a terraced garden you get a marvellous view over Eltham and beyond. Turn left to walk through a broken wall into Jack Wood, opened, like Castle Wood, to the public in 1925. Oaks, turkey oaks and sweet chestnut provide a thinnish canopy. Below these are rhododendron, holly, ferns and moss.

Keep following the wooden posts as the track climbs a gentle hill, then descends through more rhododendrons. Having crossed a narrow stream bed, walk through the rhododendrons emerging opposite Jackwood House. Turning right you walk through the gardens and, still following the posts, turn right and down into the trees.

Soon the trees part to reveal a vast meadow, Oxleas Meadow, sloping away from Shooters Hill towards the South Downs. The green meadow is darkly outlined by woods; Jack Wood to the west,

Oxleas to the east and Sheperdleas Wood to the south. To the north the tarmac path offers the best views and leads eastwards to a muddy track overhung with rhododendrons.

Signs lead right, into a clearing containing a clump of young copper beech leading into Oxleas Wood. This is an ancient wood containing mixed trees, shrubs and wildlife which attract a lot of breeding birds. Continue to follow the posts through the wood, which was coppiced until 1939 and is now being coppiced again allowing the sunlight through.

Eventually the track reaches a large crossways marked with a metal Green Chain Walk signpost. Turn left here, walking along wood chips which have successfully soaked up the wet mud. Taking the second turning to your right, and off the Green Chain trail, wander through the heart of the wood. Shooters Hill is to your left so it's best to bear right threading through the trees until you reach the stream bed which you can follow by clambering over and across its banks and then through the saplings, back to the metal signpost.

Following the sign left to Eltham Park North, turn right at the end to emerge at the southern edge of the meadows. Crossing these diagonally, through the gap at the top of the outgrown hawthorn hedge, brings you back just below Jackwood Gardens where you follow the original route back to Shooters Hill.

21 Parkland Walk

Length: 4 miles one way. Rough going but possible for wheel- and pushchairs. Food: The Shepherd's Pub in Holmesdale Road. The Parkland Walk Information Centre, 73c Stapleton Hall Road is open Thursdays 10–4, Sundays 12–5, tel. 01–341–3582. Buses: Nos 4, 19, 29, 106, 210, 221, 230, 236, 253, 279, W2, W3, W7. Underground: Finsbury Park.

The Parkland Walk is a strip of land that was once a railway and is now a young oak woodland. Had it not been for the Finsbury Park to Highgate line and the branch line to Alexandra Palace, the whole lot might otherwise have disappeared, like so much of London's land, under terraces of brick. In 1954 the last passenger train ran and in 1971 the railway tracks were removed.

From the top of the steps in Oxford Road the yellow gravelled line stretches ahead, edged with tall cow parsley, rosebay willowherb and bright yellow buttercups. Shrubs and saplings cover the banks while trees reach up and in some places over the path, like a canopied country lane. There are more than 30 different kinds of trees, 250 wildflowers and 50 birds, not to mention butterflies. Details of these and leaflets about the walk are available at the Parkland Walk Information Centre, down wooden steps on your right.

Like the trains, you go past rows of brick-walled back gardens and washing lines. The platforms of Crouch End station stand abandoned, the former footpath still leading to the local houses. The line narrows here, becoming even more rustic and suddenly opening up again where it meets the boarded-up tunnel under Shepherd's Hill.

Turn left into Holmesdale Road, and at the junction with Shepherd's Hill turn right. Cross the road and immediately before the half-timbered library turn left down a track through the trees, leading to Priory Gardens. Turn right here, and left a little while on, down a narrow alley between the houses. Marked by an elegant green cast-iron Victorian signpost, the alley leads down into Queen's Wood.

The wood is dark and deep, sliced by dazzling blades of sunlight.

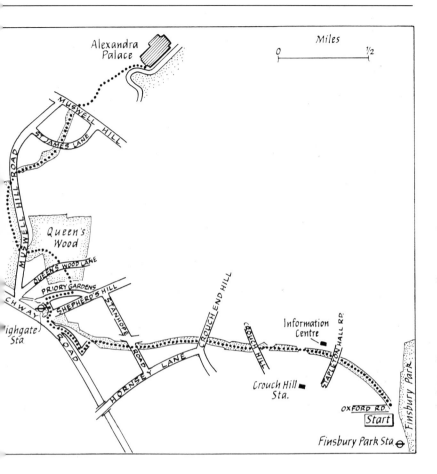

When you come to a low wall on the left, take the path bearing left and up the hill. Over the hill and down the other side is another green signpost and an elm tree whose bole sags like a heavy belly. Standing still you can hear the birds singing. Walk straight on to reach Muswell Hill Road which you cross by the red telephone box into Highgate Wood. Take the path that skirts the right-hand edge of the wood, past tall beech and oak trees, their barks striped black and green with lichen.

At the top right-hand corner of Highgate Wood you rejoin the Parkland Walk in Cranley Gardens and follow the railway line between the rooftops of Hornsey. The railway ends at the underpass where a plastic-covered walkway leads to Alexandra Park which

Disused platforms at Crouch End

contains a boating lake, formal flower gardens and an ecological garden.

Alexandra Palace crowns Muswell Hill. From the meadow slopes in front of the palace, you can watch a glistening panorama of slate-coloured roofs disappear to an infinite horizon. Built in 1873, the palace was burnt to the ground sixteen days after the official opening. It was rebuilt but caught fire again in 1980 and is now being restored as an exhibition and conference centre. A plaque commemorates the BBC television transmission mast erected here in 1936 at the beginning of regular, high-definition television. If you're feeling tired a quick way back to Finsbury Park is by the W3 bus which leaves from the road in front of the palace.

22 Plumstead Cemetery to Lesnes Abbey

Length: about 3½ miles round trip. Not suitable for push- or wheel-chairs. Food: The Abbey Café in Lesnes Abbey grounds; The For-	resters's Arms in Wickham Lane. Buses: Nos 96, 122, 122A, 422. British Rail: Abbey Wood.

This is quite a tiring walk through hilly woodland and forms part of the Green Chain Walk established by the GLC.

By Plumstead Cemetery, Cemetery Road turns into a woodland track at the base of Bostall Woods which rise fairly steeply to the north. The woods, which contain some fine beech avenues growing on a steep ridge, belonged to Sir Julian Goldsmid who sold them to the London County Council in 1893 for £12,000. Follow the Green Chain Walk's wooden posts along the well-kept path to emerge on open ground beside the bowling green on Longleigh Lane.

Heading north, across the west end of the playing fields and

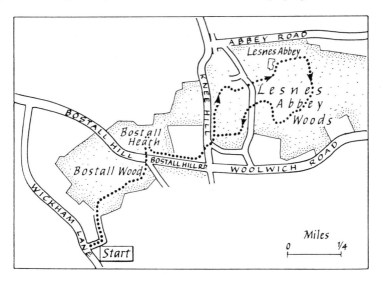

Bostall Hill Road, you enter Bostall Heath, on a wide grass clearing edged with yellow gorse in summer. The heath used to belong to Queen's College, Oxford, Lords of the Manor of Plumstead. In 1866 the College fenced the heath and attempted to sell it off. Incensed, the locals, including Goldsmid, successfully prevented the manoeuvre, only to find that the War Office marched the troops in and destroyed much of the heath's wildlife in rehearsals for the Franco-Prussian War.

The heath is not very large, but it is worth wandering north for a few hundred yards to discover a steep and thickly wooded ravine immediately to the left of the path where you might hear a woodpecker. To continue the walk, head back towards Bostall Hill Road and follow the track through the woods, bending below the branches and stepping over fallen trees until you see the red-brick chimneys of Bostall House lodge. Joining the gravel path in front of Bostall House brings you back on the Green Chain Walk.

Turn left at Knee Hill and walk down the hill about twenty-five yards to Hurst Lane where you turn right to reach the southern edge of Lesnes Abbey Woods. Take the first track on your left through the woods and head north through bluebells in spring, rhododendrons, and at the moment rather a lot of 1987 storm damage. The track eventually forks and you head east to cross another busy road, New Road, into the main part of the woods, along a path leading to Lesnes Abbey.

All that remains of the abbey are low stone walls, generally two-feet high, rising to about twelve; which is enough to imagine what it would have been. It was founded in 1178 by Richard de Luci, Chief Justiciar of England, as an act of penance for having helped rid Henry II of the troublesome Thomas à Becket. A year later Luci resigned from office and retired to spend the last three months of his life praying with the Augustinian monks at Lesnes.

Looking north from the cloister, you will see in summer the grey walls are speckled with the tiny yellow pea flowers of the black and spotted medick but the skyline is marred with square tower blocks. Looking south, beyond the formal flower gardens, all you can see are the great beech, birch, oak and sweet chestnut woods.

Walking back, take the path rising into the woods behind the remains of the Lady's Chapel. This becomes wider and skirts a fenced-off area of woodland which in early spring is swept yellow and then dusty blue with wild daffodils and bluebells. The middle of

Edge of the ravine on Bostall Heath

the wood, which contains a rich fossil bed, has been designated a Site of Special Scientific Interest. Some of the finds (a sand shark's tooth) are displayed at the Abbey Café. If you want to look for fossils you have to ask the park manager.

There are plenty of tracks through the woods. This route follows the first main track turning right, cutting through the heart of the wood. At the next junction follow the log steps up the side of a north-south running ridge and down the other side again to join the Green Chain posts and follow these back to Plumstead Cemetery.

23 Richmond Park

Length: about 4 miles. Suitable for push- and wheelchairs. Food: café at Pembroke Lodge. Information Centre, Pembroke Lodge. Buses: Nos 65, 71. British Rail and underground: Richmond.

A Londoner who has never seen the heaths and woods of Richmond, the black ponds, the brook, the bracken and moss is missing one of the joys of London.

Richmond Park in winter

All 2,358 acres of rough heathland and woods make wonderful walking. There are sweet chestnuts to gather in the autumn and bright, mahogany conkers. There are light birch copses and dark oak woods, rough briars and sharp thorns.

A good introduction to Richmond might be to start at Richmond Gate and follow the road, walking along the footpath, Hornbeam Walk, to Pembroke Lodge. Walking on a footpath when there are miles of grassland sounds dull, but it's worth it because this is the only walk in Richmond Park that offers such a splendid view and gives you so great a sense of space.

The footpath takes you along the crest of the hill on which lies the rest of the park. To the left lies Sudbrook Park, and beyond Petersham (page 28). Enter Pembroke Lodge gardens through the iron gate and turn right to walk up to Henry VIII Mound, a small steep mound that you can climb up. Standing on the top, the king is supposed to have seen the signal that Anne Boleyn had been executed.

Continue along the crest of the hill and just before you reach the road leading to Ham Lodge, below on the right, turn left. Cross the park's perimeter road and cut across country to the woods. This is the Isabella Plantation which you can enter through gates to the left.

Inside the railings, put up to keep out Richmond's famous herds of red and fallow deer, is a magnificent woodland garden at its most splendid in May when the rhododendrons and azaleas are in flower. The plantation is the only one of its kind in the park and can get overcrowded during summer weekends, but it is blissful if you get it to yourself. This walk, ending here, is one that everybody can do, but you can of course head off in any direction, or even do the eight-mile walk around the park's perimeter.

Pen Ponds, another landmark in the centre of the park, north of the Isabella Plantation, are a favourite place and the paths are well trodden. Created over two hundred years ago out of gravel pits, they are now full of carp, stickleback, roach, pike, perch and bream. Birds come here too, some to nest like mallard, great crested grebe, moorhen, coot and the inevitable Canada geese.

It's by exploring the smaller woods and copses and wandering as you will across the moors that you find the real Richmond, especially if you go early in the morning.

24 The Royal Parks

Length: about 4 miles. Fine for
push- and wheelchairs. Food: the
cafés around the Serpentine are
terrible, so take a picnic. Buses:
Nos 12, 27, 28, 31, 52, 52A, 88 to
Notting Hill; Nos 3, 11, 12, 24, 29,
53, 59, 70, 77, 88, 109, 159, 170,
177, 196 from Parliament Square.
Underground: Notting Hill Gate
or Queensway, Westminster.

'It takes London to put you in the way of a purely rustic walk from
Notting Hill to Whitehall. You may traverse this immense distance –
a most comprehensive diagonal – altogether on soft fine turf amid
the song of birds, the bleat of lambs, the ripple of ponds and the
rustle of innumerable trees.'

Henry James wrote that in 1888 and it still holds true, apart from
the lambs who went after the last war. At the beginning of the day,
when the grass is sodden and the trees shiver behind a fine mist, it
really doesn't seem possible that thousands of feet walked here the
day before.

Enter Kensington Gardens by Orme Square Gate on Bayswater
Road and walk south through the black iron gates beside the
Orangery towards Kensington Palace, designed by Christopher
Wren (and altered by Vanbrugh for George I). The first royal
occupant was King William III who bought the manor from the Earl
of Nottingham in 1689, hoping the air at Kensington would be better
for his asthma than the low ground at St James's or Whitehall.

East of the palace a square of pleached limes surrounds a sunken

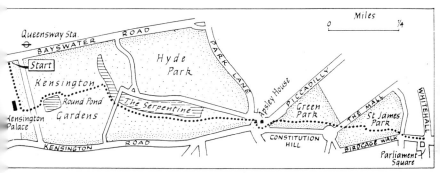

garden. From the stillness of its flower borders turn left, crossing the Broad Walk to reach the Round Pond. The wind whips up, filling the deck chairs like bloated fish. You can see across to the great dome of the Albert Hall glowing orange at dusk behind the Albert Memorial and the green copper roof of the Bandstand.

George II opened Kensington Gardens to 'well-dressed members of the public' on Saturdays. When George III moved the court to Richmond, the public were also allowed in on Sundays. It was William IV who finally opened the park to the public.

As you reach the east end of what is actually an octagonal pond, first filled with water in 1728, turn off towards G. F. Watt's statue of Physical Energy (the horse and rider). Standing here you are on a direct line from the spire of St Mary Abbots in Kensington Church Street, Princess Louise's statue of Queen Victoria (just in front of the palace) and, to the east, the Henry Moore standing like a great white bone beyond the Long Water in Hyde Park.

The Long Water is divided from the Serpentine by a bridge, designed by John Rennie in 1828. On the other side of the bridge you are in Hyde Park. Immediately the grass becomes rougher and wiry heathland takes over from the smooth green lawns of Kensington. It has seen rougher times too: duels, executions at the infamous Tyburn Corner and, today, there is Speakers Corner where political and social views are loudly aired. Charles I let the public into Hyde Park in 1637; Cromwell disapproved of the fashionable promenading and sold it off; Charles II annulled the sale and opened it up again.

As you head south-east of the Serpentine you pass Rotten Row, all that remains of the road built by William III from Kensington Palace to Whitehall, when it was lit by three hundred oil lamps. During the Great Exhibition of 1851, the Crystal Palace stood on the playing fields on your right. It was three times the size of St Paul's Cathedral and it showed 14,000 exhibits.

At the end of the Row you pass the huge statue of Achilles, cast from the iron of captured cannons and presented to the Duke of Wellington by a group of women on behalf of the ladies of England. The ladies had unwittingly commissioned the first nude statue in England. London was outraged, the ladies were embarrassed but the statue remained.

A London plane tree in Hyde Park

The yellow stone house facing Hyde Park Corner is Apsley House, No. 1 London, formerly the home of the Duke of Wellington and now a museum of his military trophies. Take the subway under Hyde Park Corner to reach Green Park. Compared with Hyde Park, it is small and informal. Tree-lined paths divide it into geometric sections. The River Tyburn flowed through here to the Mulberry Fields where James I tried to produce silk. The land was enclosed by Charles II in 1667 and known at first as Upper St James's Park. He built an ice house and walked here every day, partly for exercise and partly to see his mistress Nell Gwyn, whom he had housed in Pall Mall. His daily route became known as Constitution Hill.

Cross the Mall at the south-eastern corner of Green Park to enter St James's Park. The park was named after the hospital for leper women, founded in the thirteenth century and dedicated to St James the Less, which stood here until Henry VIII acquired the marshy land which had been used to graze swine. He drained it and built St James's Palace on the site of the hospital and within striking distance of the old royal palaces at Whitehall and Westminster. Buckingham Palace wasn't built until 1837. The Mall is technically part of St James's Park and it was along here that Charles I walked to his execution in 1649.

Charles II built a row of aviaries on the east side of the park, which became known as Birdcage Walk. He also asked for a serpentine lake to be dug, subsequently modernised by Nash in the nineteenth century. The bridge across the water is where everyone gathers to feed the birds – the sparrows and dusty pigeons as well as the exotic ducks; the pelicans tend to stay at the east end. Standing on the bridge across the lake you can see from Buckingham Palace all the way to Whitehall, the classical domes and roofs appearing romantically above the trees. From the bridge turn left to follow the lake to the south-eastern edge of the park and into Great George Street which leads to Parliament Square and Westminster underground station.

25 Wimbledon Common

Length: just over 4½ miles. Rough going with a pushchair. Wheelchairs not recommended. Food: the Windmill café, The Fox and Grapes in Camp Road. Windmill Museum: open at weekends and bank holidays, 2–5 p.m. Buses: Nos 80, 93. Underground: Southfields.

Apart from Epping Forest, Wimbledon is the largest common in London and it has belonged to the local people since 1871. It is a wild piece of land (a Site of Special Scientific Interest) that sets one wondering what London looked like before it was built.

There are whorled and rusty oaks, some bent and swollen with age, and acres of rough, heathland grasses. There are deep birch coppices that bristle with fine red twigs in winter and whistle in the summer winds. You can walk over rough gravel paths through yellow pea-flowered gorse and broom and tufts of purple heather. The air is clean enough here for curly grey-green lichens to grow and there are spongy sphagnum bogs that ooze with iron ore.

For centuries the tenants of Wimbledon Manor had the rights to graze their animals on the common and collect firewood and gravel. In 1864 Lord Spencer, Lord of the Manor of Wimbledon, tried to end the commoners' rights by enclosing the park and selling off the rest. The commoners fought this move under the leadership of Henry Peek, MP. In 1871, after a lengthy campaign, the Wimbledon and Putney Commons Act was passed and a body of eight Conservators elected to care for the land. A local rate (to pay for its upkeep) is still levied on everyone living within three-quarters of a mile of the common.

Enter the common beside a small pond beside Park Side and walk through heathland to the wide gravel Ladies' Mile. Cross this to reach a copse of gnarled oaks. The spongy moss underfoot is a brilliant green. This track joins a gravelled cycle path, Windmill Ride North. Turn left on to this and walk past a grassy tumulus, at the top of which is a stone monument commemorating the 300th anniversary of the Tangier Regiment of Foot, later the Queen's

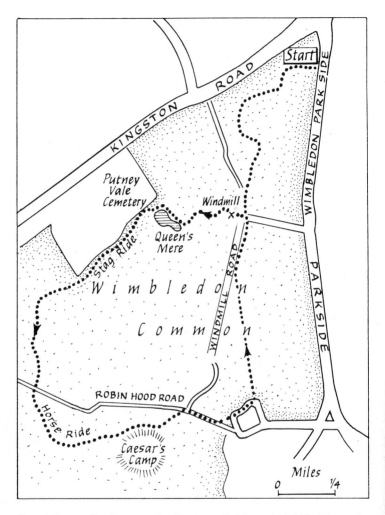

Royal Surrey Regiment, who first paraded here in 1661. Throughout the common there are butts (earth embankments to catch bullets) from the days when the National Rifle Association held their meetings here. This came to an end in 1887 when a gravedigger in Putney Vale Cemetery was accidentally shot by a stray bullet and the NRA moved to Bisley. You might see a small, brown kestrel hovering and watching for prey here – just one of over eighty different kinds of bird that have been seen on the Common.

Continue along Windmill Ride North, which joins Windmill Road leading south to the windmill, built in 1817 by Charles Marsh, who was a carpenter not a miller, which might explain the mill's unusual design. Inside is the Windmill Museum. The sixteen chimneys that you can see from the outside date from the 1860s when Earl Spencer persuaded the Marsh family to move and converted the small mill into a home for six families.

Leaving the windmill, walk past the café and the London Scottish Golf Club and follow the earth track on the right down into the wood ahead. On the left is a dry stream bed, on the right hawthorn, holly and ivy; smooth grey beech and rough oaks grow on top of the mossy banks.

At the bottom of the hill is Queen's Mere, a large pond, made at the end of the 1800s by damming a bog. Bald, white-headed coots and tufted duck nest here. In spring you might find some frog spawn and water boatmen skimming along the shallow surface at the south edge. Walk past marsh plants – flat, round-leafed marsh pennywort and tall marsh willowherb to the north end of the pond – and follow the path that leads down through the mixed wood and rough undergrowth until you reach Stag Ride. Ahead is Putney Vale

A mere on the Common

Cemetery. Turn left here and follow the path through more woods. On the right you can see a wooded hill in Richmond Park.

Just after the track bends left you cross over another track and keep going through high old beech and oak. Follow the horse ride until it joins Robin Hood Road. Then bear left along a grassy track to North View, distinguished by tall red-brick Victorian houses. If you follow this road round to the right into Camp Road you will find The Fox and Grapes.

From the northern corner of West Place follow a track north, across a horse ride. The track then bears slightly left to run beside Windmill Road. Where Windmill Road turns right, continue beyond it to join Ladies' Mile and retrace your steps back to the start of the walk.

STREET WALKS

26 Brick Lane and Columbia Road

Length: 3 miles there and back.
Food: the bagel café in Ezra
Street; there are cafés, pubs,
Indian restaurants everywhere.

Buses: Nos 5, 10, 15, 15A, 22A,
25, 40, 67, 225, 253. Underground: Aldgate East.

Try to do this walk on a spring Sunday morning. Sunday is the only day Brick Lane and Columbia Road markets open and spring is the best time for the Columbia Road flowers.

From Aldgate East station, turn left along Whitechapel Road, walking past Bloom's restaurant, the most famous kosher restaurant in Britain. Turn left into Osborn Street which becomes Brick Lane, where bricks were made in the sixteenth century. The Lane was developed from the southern end upwards in the seventeenth century and is now the heart of London's East End Bengali community.

Indian sailors settled in Spitalfields at the end of the eighteenth century and the first Bengalis came a hundred years later. They followed three hundred years of immigration by Huguenots, Irish Catholics and Jews who introduced and established the clothing trade in Spitalfields. There are workshops everywhere, particularly at the top of Brick Lane.

Indian music wafts across the Lane from shop fronts plastered with garish yellow video posters and mixes with the smell of cumin and coriander from the neighbouring restaurants. Elegant Indian mannequins in purple and silver, red and gold speckled saris stare aloofly from another shop window. An Asian pulls up his van and opens the back doors. After discussions with a group of friends who suddenly appear from the alleys, he starts selling boxes of fruit at half price. But half of what?

The large stone pedimented chapel at the corner of Fournier Street is the London Jamme Masjid. It was originally built in 1743 for the Huguenots. It became a synagogue in 1898 and is now a

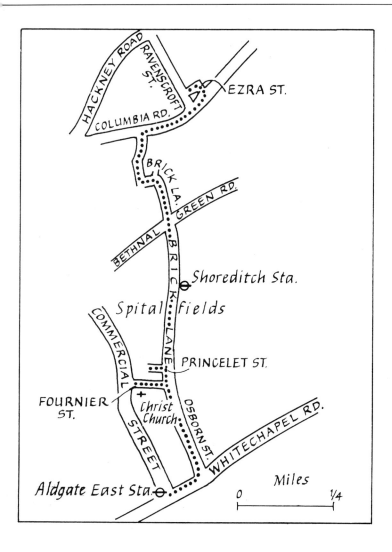

mosque. Looking up you might be able to tell the time by the sundial. Take a detour down Fournier Street, originally Church Street, which was developed in the 1720s on the then green fields of Spital. The houses are brick, beautifully proportioned, some with fine stucco porches. The weatherboarded garrets were designed to offer as much light as possible to the cloth weavers who moved in after the wealthy families left. Many of the windows are dusty and dark, with

Shop in Brick Lane

the occasional furriers' and clothiers' signs still up. No. 14 is particularly fine. To the right above the door, you can see a small lead fire protection badge belonging to the Phoenix Assurance Company. On the opposite house, No. 37, is another lead badge with a sun sign.

The fine white spire of Nicholas Hawksmoor's Christ Church towers at the end of the street above Spitalfields Market (shut on Sundays). This was one of the results of the Fifty New Churches Act of 1711 passed by the new High Church Tory government and, despite Victorian alterations, it remains as perhaps the finest of Hawksmoor's churches. It was first used by the Huguenots, many of whom are buried in the graveyard.

Back in Brick Lane, almost immediately opposite is Ch. N. Katz's shop with two iron signs advertising his wares: 'String, twine, cord and paper bags' reads one; 'Brown paper, corrugated, waterproof, tissue, gum' the other. Continuing along Brick Lane take another detour left at Princelet Street which contains more eighteenth-century houses. No. 13 has been restored but still retains its small lead badge. The two houses ahead of you in Wilkes Street have wooden shutters and though lived in today, their dark windows and black doors belong to the past.

Back in Brick Lane you soon pass Truman's Black Eagle Brewery, established at the end of the seventeenth century. Nos 65–79 were built by Joseph Truman in 1706. On the right you can see Truman's brick chimney with 'Truman' in white lettering. The brewery was restored in 1976. On the corner with Buxton Street is The Two Old Brewers, established in 1666.

In the brick tunnel by Shoreditch underground station is a grubby secondhand market; so desperate that the traders sell blunt used pencils and inky biros at 5 pence each. Emerging from the tunnel you suddenly find yourself in the midst of a great throng of people, market stalls, helium balloons, boxes of mangoes, grapes or whatever is in season. Looking above and left at the corner of Sclater Street you can see the original stone plaque engraved, 'This is Sclater Street.'

Fighting on north, just before you reach the junction with Bethnal Green Road look out for the excellent bagel shops on the left, where batches of fresh bagels are constantly being turned out. Cross the road and continue along the Lane. On the right-hand side in Padbury Court is a small two-storey red-brick terrace, the Quaker Square workshops.

At the end of the Lane turn left through the modern estate and right into Columbia Road, where shelves of flowers rise above the car roofs. There are some interesting shops in the Victorian terrace on the right selling dried flowers, secondhand books, cockles and whelks etc. The road is filled with people carrying trayloads of garden and window plants and wheeling bicycles strung with bunches of flowers.

Turn left into Ezra Street which leads over cobbles to a small area by an old-fashioned cheese and grocer's shop and on the left a pottery yard. Straight ahead, in the narrow alley, a former cow barn is being used as a café selling tea and coffee from the pot and freshly prepared bagels with cream cheese and salmon, which you must try.

27 Brompton Cemetery

Length: about ¾ mile. Fine for push- and wheelchairs. Brompton Cemetery is open daily from 9 a.m. (10 a.m. on Sundays) and closes at 7 p.m. No dogs allowed. Buses: Nos 14, 30, 31, 74, 264. Underground: West Brompton or Earl's Court.

On a Saturday afternoon in Brompton Cemetery you can sit in the sun, resting against a gravestone shrouded with ivy, as if you were in the middle of nowhere. That is until the roar of the crowd from Chelsea football ground reminds you of the real world. The cemetery's now closed for burials and is used by local people as somewhere to walk and while away the time in the shadow of stone angels.

The cemetery at Brompton was one of half a dozen built by the government to try and cope with serious overcrowding in London graveyards. Consecrated in 1840, by 1889 over 150,000 people had been buried in forty acres of land, the numbers being swollen by the 14,000 London victims of the cholera epidemic in 1849. In summer a crowd of tilted gravestones and monuments can just be seen through a mist of cow parsley.

Entering by the south gate in Fulham Road you walk towards a brilliant copper beech which overhangs the large square tomb of Robert Coombes, champion sculler, who died in 1860. The sheer size of this tomb, easily taller than the man himself and guarded at the four corners by now-headless footmen, is just a taste of what is to come. Rich and poor alike, the Victorians went to great lengths to give their relatives a 'proper' resting place.

The memorial architecture ranges from baroque to neo-classical, rustic to Egyptian. Tombs, vaults, monuments, plinths, pedestals, statues and crosses are arranged in rectangular plots around the classical yellow stone catacombs and chapel, designed by Benjamin Baud.

Many of the soft sandstone monuments have blackened and weathered away leaving leprous remains, and most of the copper railings have been removed, but for all that the cemetery looks more

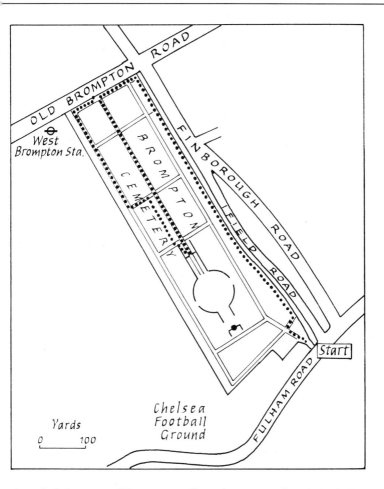

dignified than ever. The grass is allowed to grow tall and bluebells, purple vetch and pink herb robert grow between the graves and beside the paths. The strength of the prehistoric horsetail, a jointed primeval plant, is such that it can push up through the tarmac paths. There are fine trees too: yew, beech, sycamore and plane.

When you reach the north boundary with Old Brompton Road turn left and walk to the central avenue, marked by two vast family mausoleums on the right. Turn down here passing on the left two great angels and next to them a boy and girl, dressed in sailor suit and frock, standing at the head of their father's grave. A few yards further on the left is the grave of the suffragette leader, Emmeline Pankhurst

A gravestone

(1857–1928), marked by a tall red sandstone Celtic cross with an austere relief of Christ by Eric Gill (1882–1940).

Continue south over three paths to find perhaps the finest memorial in this cemetery, a decorated copper tomb, now eau-de-Nil, designed by Edward Burne-Jones for Frederick Leyland, patron of the Pre-Raphaelites. This is flanked by a Gothic sarcophagus made of Siennese marble for Leyland's son-in-law, the artist Val Prinsep, R.A.

When you reach the main catacombs, wander around them and then head west to the boundary wall. Peering through the black iron gates barring the entrance to the catacombs in the west boundary wall, one can make out in the dusty dark the crumbling remains of forgotten coffins.

Turn right and walk north along the eastern perimeter. At the top on your right is a monument to the Chelsea Pensioners.

You can either leave by the Old Brompton Road gate, turning left to find West Brompton underground station, or wander back to Fulham Road.

28 Chelsea to Battersea

Length: 3 miles round trip. Fine for wheel- and pushchairs. The Royal Hospital Chapel, Great Hall, Museum and gardens are open every weekday from 10–12 a.m. and from 2 p.m. till dusk. On Sundays they open from 2 p.m. The Chelsea Physic Garden is open on Wednesday and Sunday afternoons from mid-April to mid-October between 2.00 p.m. and 5.00 p.m. Tel. 01–352–5646. Food: cafeteria in Battersea Park; tea at the Physic Garden. Bus: No. 39 to the Embankment. Underground: Sloane Square or South Kensington are nearest but both are about a mile away.

Just over a hundred years ago, the Chelsea riverside was the centre of a village. In 1874 Joseph Bazalgette built the Embankment to cover the gigantic new sewage complex he had designed for London. Black stone walls, pavement and tarmac now cover the country lane and the trees which once leant over the mudflats where boats were

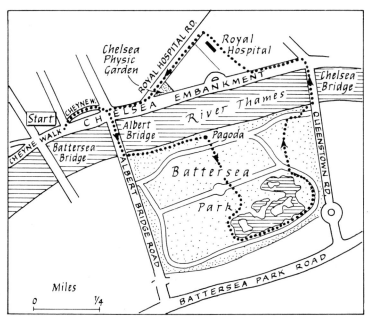

hauled up out of the water. Amid the surge of traffic the only echoes from the past are the barges moored at Chelsea Reach that rise and fall with the tide as gulls mewl and wheel in the wind like lost scraps of paper.

From Chelsea Old Church walk east, between the statue of Thomas More and the church garden's railings. In the corner of the gardens stands a white stone monument to Hans Sloane. Doctor, writer, collector, naturalist, this extraordinary man succeeded Isaac Newton to the presidency of the Royal Society, was physician to the Queen, physician-general to the army and benefactor to the Chelsea Physic Garden. His name appears all over Chelsea (Sloane Square, Hans Crescent).

Sloane brought his collection of plants, curios and books to Chelsea in 1743 and moved into Chelsea Manor. The manor, which stood on the site of 19–26 Cheyne Walk, had been built by Henry VIII when Chelsea was the 'Village of Palaces'. After Sloane's death, Baron Cadogan of Oakley pulled it down and built the tall red-brick houses that are there today.

Turn left into Cheyne Walk, where Rossetti, Swinburne and Meredith lived in No. 16. Rossetti's caterwauling collection of peacocks caused such a fuss that a new no-bird clause was written into the lease of the house. No. 5 belonged to John Camden Neild, a miser, who left £500,000 to Queen Victoria in his will, which she used to help build Balmoral.

Cross Albert Bridge, built in 1873 by R. M. Ordish, the architect of the roof of the Albert Hall, to reach Battersea Park. Turn left and walk along the riverside, through the avenue of mature planes. Before Battersea Park was created by an Act of Parliament in 1846 Battersea Fields were rough marsh lands, threaded with black streams and ditches that flooded at every high tide. Battersea's notorious Red House Tavern had become the centre of the infamous Sunday Fairs. Gypsies camped here in the summer and conjurors, tricksters, hawkers and vendors met with dancers, horse and donkey racers, fortune tellers and gamblers in a bawdy, drunken rabble. The government closed the inns in the 1840s and asked James Pennethorne to design a park.

The Bhuddist Peace Pagoda was built beside the river in 1985 by the Nipponzan Myohoji Bhuddists. At the pagoda turn right and walk down steps into the formal gardens towards the lake. Walking anti-clockwise round the water you pass statues by Nicola Hicks,

The willow-pattern tree

Henry Moore and Barbara Hepworth. As you approach the low round cafeteria building you pass on the right a hilly field of wallabies, rabbits, deer and peacocks.

Walk past the sports ground to the exit by Chelsea Bridge, passing on the way a fenced conservation area, planted with native trees, wildflowers and bulbs to attract the wildlife which disappeared after many fences and shrubs were pulled out.

Cross the bridge and turn left to reach Ranelagh Gardens, famous pleasure gardens in the eighteenth century. Turning right at the gates walk along the path to the Royal Hospital, commissioned by Charles II after seeing the Hôtel des Invalides in Paris. Christopher Wren was asked to design a similar asylum for veteran soldiers. The building was finished in 1691 and 420 pensioners now live there, wearing the navy blue and scarlet uniforms, designed in the eighteenth century.

Turn left into Royal Hospital Road and left again into Swan Walk, where the entrance to the Chelsea Physic Garden stands opposite four delightful eighteenth-century houses with exclusive views over the high brick wall of the Physic Garden. The garden was founded in

1673 by the Worshipful Society of Apothecaries in the belief that all plants were of use to man and had been put on Earth by God for that reason. Gardens like this had been used since the mid-sixteenth century and this was the second garden in Britain of its kind. Now, it is the last, producing the plants needed for teaching and research as well as preserving rare species. It was closed to the public in 1899 for nearly a hundred years until 1983.

Combining vital research into the effects of air pollution with the running of an English country garden is some achievement. In summer swathes of bright colour fill the borders, which contain varieties of roses, sweet peas and daisies planted by species. In one corner are the plants from Asia and South America; in another the medicinal and poisonous plants – henbane, mandrake, double bloodroot and monkshood. Rows of feverfew form part of an experiment to discover whether the old wives' tale that feverfew can help migraine sufferers is true.

At the southern end is a rock garden, the first in the country. It was made in 1772 with basaltic lava from Iceland. In early summer clusters of tiny wild strawberries are found all over the garden.

29 Covent Garden

Length: just over 1½ miles. Food: there are cafés, restaurants and pubs in most streets. Buses: Nos 1, 14, 19, 22, 24, 29, 38, 55, 176 to Cambridge Circus. Underground: Covent Garden.

Covent Garden stands on the site of a medieval Benedictine Abbey (or Convent). John Russell, 1st Earl of Bedford, inherited the land after the dissolution of the monasteries. The 4th Earl obtained planning permission from Charles I and engaged Inigo Jones. Inspired by the Italians, Jones designed a kind of piazza – an open square surrounded by stone colonnades leading to shops and above these three-storey terrace houses. Thus London's first square was built between 1633 and 1637. At the west end Inigo Jones placed his church, St Paul's.

Walking south from the underground along James Street, you pass on your left the back of the Royal Opera House. Walk on towards the central market building, designed in 1830. Jones's piazza attracted fruit- and flowersellers, and in 1670 the Bedfords were granted the right by Royal Charter to hold a regular market for fruit, flowers, roots and herbs, charging traders a toll.

By the 1750s more permanent sheds were erected. As the market flourished, the fashionable families moved to the smarter area around St James's and many of their homes were converted into Turkish baths and/or brothels. Actors and artists moved in, accompanied by several new coffee houses.

By the 1830s a permanent market building was erected to instil some order into the market. The wrought-iron and glass Floral Hall which you can see at the east end of the piazza was built in 1872 and now houses the London Transport Museum.

In 1974 Covent Garden market moved to Nine Elms. Covent Garden was restored and is now crammed with shops selling everything from clothes and accessories, to food, household goods and books. There are still market stalls and street performers on the cobblestones at the east and west ends of the piazza.

At the east end of the market, turn into Russell Street walking past

Boswell's Coffee House, where Boswell first met Dr Johnson. A black board inside tells the tale. At Bow Street turn left, passing on the right Bow Street Police Station and Magistrates' Court. Henry Fielding, the novelist and barrister, was the second Bow Street magistrate and in 1753 established the Bow Street Runners.

Directly opposite are the imposing classical features of the Royal Opera House, which first opened in 1732. Turn right into Broad Court past the bronze of a seated ballerina and walk through the flats to Drury Lane. At the junction with Great Queen Street, if you look right, you can see the Freemasons' Hall built like some vast stone liner in 1927–33.

Walking north along Drury Lane there is little to look at now. The first Sainsbury's opened in 1869 on the site of the New London Theatre. It is worth continuing across the busy intersection with High Holborn to reach Museum Street which contains some lovely Georgian and early Victorian shops, the Atlantis Bookshop, Blooms-bury Rare Books and some cheap cafés. The British Museum stands in front of you in Great Russell Street. Gosh!, The London Comic Shop, is just beyond the junction with Coptic Street.

Turn left and left again down Coptic Street, passing the Pizza Express which has taken over a Victorian brick building, formerly The Dairy Supply Company Limited. Cross New Oxford Street, using the zebra crossing on the right, and look in the windows of James Smith and Sons, umbrella and stick specialists, which is on the corner of Shaftesbury Avenue. Opened in 1867, the shop windows are framed with gleaming brass and the original painted-glass surrounds.

Walk down Shaftesbury Avenue, past the Shaftesbury Theatre and cross over to Endell Street. The Protestant Eglise Suisse (1854) is on the right and further along is the British Central Cleaning Company in a narrow and deserted Victorian building, the dirtiest in the street. Sandwiched between two good-looking French restaurants, Mon Marché and Mélange, is Latchford's Timber Yard, an attractive brick and stucco building still used by Latchford's. On the corner with Shorts Gardens is a good fish-and-chip restaurant, The Rock and Sole Plaice, with tables on the wide pavement outside.

Before turning right into Shorts Gardens look at No. 22 Endell Street, formerly Lavers and Barrand Stained Glass Works, a long, decorated red-brick building with pointed and flattened arched windows. At Neal Street turn right, walking up to the junction with

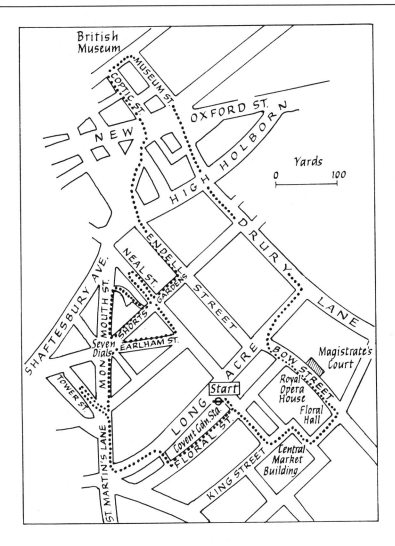

Monmouth Street and down the other side. There are so many shop windows to look at: Franks Café, The Hat Shop, Rayman Eastern Musical Instruments, The Kite Store, Astrohome.

Back at the junction with Shorts Gardens turn right past Nos 21–23, Neal's Yard Wholefood Warehouse. If you look up you can see the mechanical clock which chimes the hours. Turning right through the passage you reach Neal's Yard, a triangle of cobbles

The Central Market building

surrounded by early nineteenth-century brick houses selling whole-foods, organic produce and delicious vegetarian meals which people eat sitting or standing around the yard.

The covered passageway at the other end of the yard brings you out on Monmouth Street opposite the Nouvel Hôpital et Dispensaire Français. Monmouth Street market was famous in the last century for secondhand clothes. Turn left and on the left-hand side of the street is another good French restaurant, Mon Plaisir, and at No. 27 the Monmouth Coffee House which sells the best coffee beans. You can sample the coffee at the back of the shop.

At Shorts Gardens turn left and then right down the next section of Neal Street which is packed with more shops. Where Neal Street joins Shelton Street, at the corner of Earlham Street, there is usually a gathering of people, particularly when The Crown and Anchor is open. Turn right up Earlham Street, past the Donmar Warehouse to Seven Dials. This was conceived by Thomas Neale, Master of the Mint. In the middle stood a Doric column topped with a seven-dial clock from which radiated seven streets. In 1773 the pillar was removed because of a rumour that there was a pile of money below it.

There wasn't. The circular cobblestone area you see today was laid down only within the last few years.

Turning left and walking down Monmouth Street you pass the tiled exterior of The Two Brewers (1933) and opposite, No. 67, which is in the process of being restored. A faded advertisement on the brick reads, 'Saddle and Harness Maker, established 1847'; but I doubt it will survive the restoration. Looking down the hill towards Trafalgar Square, you can see St Martin-in-the-Fields. If you walk up Tower Street you will find Dobell's famous Jazz and Folk Record Shop, and round the side, Tower Court, a pretty cul-de-sac with tubs of flowers outside the houses.

Continuing down Monmouth Street turn left into Long Acre, once a narrow strip of land belonging to the Benedictine monks and developed at the beginning of the seventeenth century. It is now a mixture of modern, Georgian and Victorian buildings. Conduit Court, just after Stanford's map shop, the largest in the world, leads through to Floral Street. The white Italianate building (1860) used to be a school and is now The Fitness Centre. In 1842 the building next door was a brothel and five years later a cowhouse. The Tin Tin shop is at No. 34. At the end of Floral Street, turn left to get back to the underground.

30 Fleet Street to Smithfield

Length: just over 1½ miles one way. Food: the cafés and pubs in Fleet Street; the pubs in Cloth Fair – some of the best; or try the Snackbox, a small eat-in or take-away café in Kinghorn Street. Buses: Nos 4, 6, 9, 11, 15, 171A, 502, 509, 513. Underground: Aldwych (sometimes closed), Temple.

The River Fleet still flows under Farringdon Street as a sewer spewing into the Thames, probably smelling no worse than it did in the Middle Ages when sewage and refuse were regularly thrown in. The Fleet rises in the Hampstead ponds and the name, meaning tidal inlet, originally referred only to its lower reaches.

With the arrival in about 1500 of Wynkyn de Worde, who set up business under the sign of The Sun at the end of Shoe Lane, Fleet Street printing and publishing were established. Starting at Temple Bar at the beginning of Fleet Street you will see some interesting buildings on both sides of the street. No. 17 is the half-timbered entrance to the Inner Temple (page 153). No. 22 is Ye Olde Cock Tavern, built in 1887 to replace a sixteenth-century inn; its half-timbered front is barely ten feet wide. No. 29 is an elaborate piece of Victorian stucco work, interspersed with pink granite columns and fiddly decoration.

On the north side, if you peer into Hen and Chickens Court, you will find a tiny courtyard, shadowed by tall nineteenth-century buildings. Further on, St Dunstan in the West has at its east end, embedded in a blue niche above the vestry door, the statue of Queen Elizabeth I which stood on Ludgate until it was demolished in 1760.

Though fast disappearing, the newspaper world is still here in El Vino's wine bar; the Reuters building, designed by Lutyens; the London News Agency; the Dundee Courier. The black glass and chrome *Daily Express* building, nicknamed the Black Lubianka, is at No. 121. But the *Daily Telegraph* building at No. 135 is closed now and old mail lies in a dusty heap at the entrance.

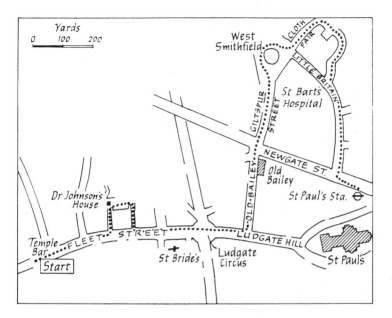

Johnson's Court leads to Gough Square and Dr Johnson's house, built in 1700. The contents are for those with a real interest in the life of the diarist, but it is delightful to wander through the sloping rooms, up the creaking staircase to the attic. On the first-floor landing is a contemporary map of St James's Park showing the Long Water and on the second landing a glass case contains a brick from the Great Wall of China.

Leaving Gough Square (Johnson spelt it Goff) from its east end via Hind Court, you walk past the Cheshire Cheese, a famous oak-beamed watering hole visited by Johnson and Boswell, Garrick, Reynolds and later, Dickens, Tennyson, Carlyle and Wilkie Collins. On the right is a timbered newsagent's.

Back in Fleet Street, St Bride's Church, on the right, built by Wren to replace the fifteenth-century perpendicular church burnt down in the Great Fire, is topped by the tallest of his steeples. Wren's wedding-cake tiers of octagonal arcades so inspired an eighteenth-century baker, Mr Rich, that he became famous for his wedding cakes of St Bride's. The church's crypt is a museum containing the remains of a Roman house excavated after an air raid in 1940. The excavations revealed a number of Celtic artefacts,

Bartholomew Close

supporting the legend that the sixth-century Irish Saint, Bridget, founded the first Christian church on this spot.

Walking downhill you reach Ludgate Circus, built in 1875 on the site of the old Fleet Bridge. Only two sections of the circus remain. In a house near the bridge the first daily newspaper, the *Daily Courant*, was opened in 1702.

To your left Farringdon Street is spanned by the massive Holborn Viaduct, built in 1869 with the pomp and circumstance of solid Victorian iron work. Continue up Ludgate Hill, named after King Lud's Gate which is thought to have been built in 66 BC. Like other City gates, it was pulled down in 1760.

Turn left to walk up Old Bailey, the street to reach the Old Bailey, the Central Criminal Court on the site of Newgate Prison. In the Middle Ages the condemned were hanged immediately after conviction and the relatives would have to rush forward to prevent the bodysnatchers from stealing the body.

Crossing the end of Holborn Viaduct you enter Giltspur Street, previously called Knightrider Street because medieval knights galloped up here to the great tournaments held at Smithfield. On the left-hand corner stands the Church of St Sepulchre, founded in 1137. St Sepulchre was built, like the Holy Sepulchre in Jerusalem, without the north-west gate of the City and from here the crusaders set off on their journeys to the Holy City. The church has suffered much damage and restoration. Bodysnatching from the graveyard became such a problem that a watchhouse (which you can still see) was built by the gates in Giltspur Street.

The corner of Cock Lane is one of many places where the Great Fire of London stopped and is marked by a small gilded statue of a boy. A notice in the window recalls that the bodysnatchers used to dump bodies in the building that stood here. The thief's name was attached to the corpse so that the surgeons from St Bartholomew's Hospital opposite knew who to pay.

St Bartholomew's Hospital, on the right, founded in the twelfth century and the oldest in London, survived Henry VIII, although the associated priory was dissolved. A statue of Henry stands above the pale stone 1702 gateway at the top right-hand side of Giltspur Street. William Harvey was chief physician here in 1609–33 and William Hogarth, appointed governor in 1734, bequeathed the hospital two of his paintings which still hang here.

Smithfield, originally 'Smoothfield', a large grassy space just outside the City walls, was the site of a horse market in the twelfth century. It was also used for royal tournaments and public executions and cattle, pig and sheep fairs were held here. Bartholomew Fair was established in 1123 by Rahere, Henry I's court minstrel, who, having survived malaria, vowed to reform his ways. Henry gave him the land to build a priory and hospital (St Bartholomew's). It soon became the biggest cloth fair in Britain. It started on the eve of St Bartholomew's Day and lasted three days during which Rahere, even in his reformed Augustinian days, would join in with his juggling tricks.

By 1855 Bartholomew Fair had grown out of hand. Cattle, terrified by the smell of blood, stampeded through the streets and into shops. Dickens described it in *Oliver Twist*: 'the ground was covered, nearly ankle-deep, with filth and mire.' The fair was replaced in 1856 by Smithfield Market.

Walking through Smithfield during the day, hours after the morning market is over, a galling stench sticks in the air. Steel-sharp meat hooks hang from the wrought-iron roof, thick as spines. From a vast refrigerated lorry bright red blood drips on to the fresh sawdust.

From the market buildings head east to reach St Bartholomew the

Great, the oldest parish church in London, founded in 1123 by Rahere. An arched half-timbered gatehouse, only discovered during the First World War when bomb damage shook off modern plaster to reveal the timbers, leads along a flagstone passage to the church doors. In the sixteenth century Henry VIII closed the priory, and the church has at various times since then housed a blacksmith's forge, printer's workshops, a school, a carpenter's workshop and also stored hops.

Cloth Fair to the left of the church contains two of the oldest houses in London and some excellent old pubs. The top end of the street has been recently and successfully rebuilt and several houses now contain small offices. Turning right into Kinghorn Street and Bartholomew Close, where a dusty Dickensian haberdashery store still stands beside a building site, brings you to Little Britain. The plain Victorian warehouses here are now being systematically destroyed to make room for out-of-scale modern developments. With just a handful of residents in the City it seems that there is no one to stop the developers' greed.

Opposite the National Postal Museum in King Edward Street is Postman's Park, the old graveyard of St Botolph's Church. St Botolph is the patron saint of travellers and the church stood outside Aldersgate, the northern entrance to the medieval City of London. A plaque on the buildings opposite the church marks the position of the gate. Inside the sizeable graveyard stands G. F. Watt's tiled wall, dedicated to men and women who died saving another's life in 1900. The true stories, taken from newspapers, are preserved on glazed tiles beneath a small shelter.

From the park it is a short walk up Newgate Street – avoiding the soulless modern shopping precinct – to St Paul's underground station.

31 Hampstead Village

Length: about 1 mile. Fairly hilly, not suitable for wheelchairs. Food: The Holly Bush Hotel, Holly Bush Hill; Burgh House in New End Square serves coffee, lunch and tea (closed on Monday and Tuesday). Fenton House is open Wednesday – Saturday 11 a.m.–5 p.m., Sunday 2–5 p.m. Bus: No. 268. Underground: Hampstead.

The best thing about Hampstead Village is the nonsensical way the lanes skew round the story-book hill. They head up here, dragging

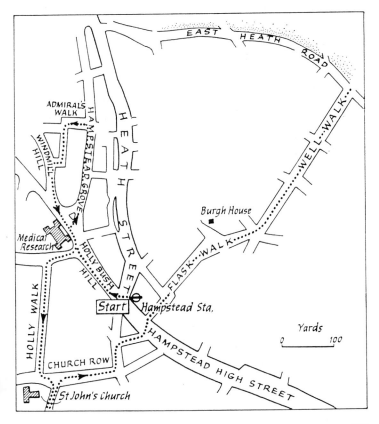

you with them, then for no good reason, double back down, yards from where they started. Round every corner there's a surprise, so that walking around the village ends up as confusing as a game of snakes and ladders.

The story of the village is punctuated by the discovery in the eighteenth century of a iron-rich spring in Well Walk which soon had fashionable Londoners flocking to taste the waters and dance in the Pump and Assembly Rooms. In 1850 the pompously titled survey *A Microscopic Examination of the Water Supplied to the Inhabitants of London* discovered all kinds of hidden horrors in the water. The crowds thinned, but Hampstead, enriched by its iron spa, has never looked back.

Coming out of Hampstead underground, climb Holly Hill. The cornerhouse on the right stands on the site of the old clock tower. On the left-hand side, by the entrance to the school, the pavement bears left behind railings to Mount Vernon. On an old, curved brick wall you'll see the first of the Hampstead street signs written in white on glazed brown tiles with white script. This is how all the old road names are marked here.

Turn right here and follow the railings down and round to Holly Bush Hill and the Holly Bush Hotel. Bear right at the triangle of grass ahead, past the lovely white weatherboarded cottage where George Romney lived. The wrought-iron gates at the entrance to the grounds of Fenton House, built in 1693, were made by Jean Tijou. Beside the high brick wall of Fenton House, which contains an historic collection of instruments including a 1612 harpsichord reputedly used by Handel, stands such an elegant lamp post.

The next large house on the right was lived in by George Du Maurier. Turn left down Admiral's Walk, named after Admiral Matthew Barton who lived in Hampstead in the eighteenth century. Fairly wide and rural, it leads down the hill past the large white Admiral's House which has a quarterdeck on the roof and was the home of the architect George Gilbert Scott. In the low white cottage next door, Grove Lodge, John Galsworthy wrote *The Forsyte Saga*.

Opposite Admiral's House a track leads through bushes and back gardens to Windmill Hill. Turn left here, walking back down to the bottom of Holly Bush Hill. Bear right along the path up the hill to the Mount Vernon junction and this time continue round the brick wall (don't go down Holly Hill) and eighteenth-century terrace. Robert Louis Stevenson lived in the house at the corner of Holly Walk.

Frognal Way

Turn left here and you can see at the bottom of the hill St John's Church against a distant grey skyline. Going downhill, you have to keep stopping to look at the houses and cottages on the left. At the corner of Hollyberry Lane stands the house where the first Hampstead Police Force began their nightly watches in the 1830s. A little further down on the left is a short terrace, Holly Place, built in 1816, in the centre of which stands the pretty little Catholic Church of St Mary, founded by the Abbé Morel for French refugees and looking as if one were suddenly in some quiet corner of France. The church has a small open bellcote above a statue of the Virgin, carved from Caen stone.

Benham's Place was built in 1813. From the simple cottages front gardens lead to a narrow flagged and guttered alley, opposite two weatherboarded detached villas in Prospect Place. Colour-washed pink and green they ought to be standing above the shingle of an English beach, not overlooking an overgrown churchyard. Continuing down Holly Walk turn left into Church Row opposite St John's Church where Constable and Du Maurier are buried.

A few yards further on the right of Frognal Way, make a detour down to the bollards at the end to look at the backs of the eighteenth-century houses in Church Row. Then go back and walk along Church Row towards Heath Street. The houses on the south side were built in 1720. The houses on the north side are all mixed styles and periods. Halfway along is a white weatherboarded cottage with an oversailing bay.

Cross Heath Street on the zebra crossing and walk along Oriel Place where there is a tiny garden, beside Baker's Passage, no bigger than the spreading branches of the tree in the middle of it, encircled by a wrought-iron seat. At the end of Oriel Place cross Hampstead High Street at the zebra crossing and continue along Flask Walk.

This flagstone alley is lined with shops and the Flask Tavern, with a Victorian tiled exterior. At the end of the Walk, look up Back Lane on your left with its pretty terrace of brick cottages rising up the hill. When you reach the small triangle of grass, look left to find the Wells and Campden Baths built of red brick in 1888.

Gardnor House, a square brick house built in 1736 and surrounded by a brick wall, is on your right. Burgh House stands near the junction with New End Square. Built in 1703, it is let at a peppercorn rent to the Burgh House Trust who run exhibitions, a local museum and organise concerts.

Continuing along Well Walk, you pass Wells Tavern on the right. A red sign tells you about Hampstead spring.

Further along on the left-hand side is a fountain and on the right John Constable's house. Well Walk leads to Hampstead Heath, and via the avenue opposite, Parliament Hill, where you can go on to explore the heath or return.

32 Mayfair

Length: 2 miles. Food: the nicest and cheapest places to eat are in Shepherd Market. Buses: Nos 9, 14, 19, 22, 25, 38, 509. Underground: Green Park.

Mayfair is like a beautiful tart: unaffordable except by the very rich. But it costs nothing to look.

The May Fair, held here every year from 1686 to 1764, began on the first of May and lasted through fifteen riotous days of acrobats, performing animals, betting, racing and circus tricks.

Coming out of the northern exit from Green Park station, turn right and then right again, down Half Moon Street, once the home of

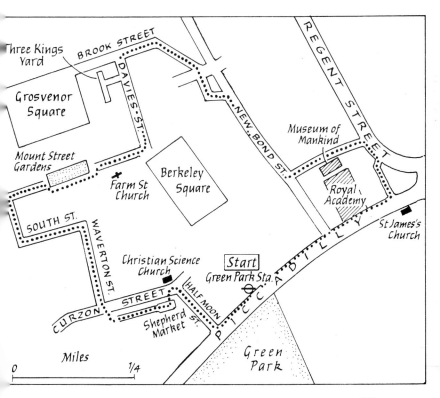

Davies Street

James Boswell, Lola Montez and Somerset Maugham. There are several Georgian houses here, but the street is dominated by the great white Third Church of Christ Scientist (1910–12).

Turn left into Curzon Street walking past the eau-de-Nil and white stucco jeweller's shop and left through the covered passage into Shepherd Market, the site of the old May Fair. The Shepherd was Edward Shepherd, the architect who developed Mayfair at the end of the seventeenth century.

Around the small market square tables and chairs are set out on the pavements as if a continental sun shone down here. Cross Trebeck Street and continue past Tiddy Dol's Eating House where a plaque outside tells you about Tiddy Dol, the gingerbread man. Turning right up Hertford Street, cross Curzon Street into Chesterfield Street, one of the best-preserved Georgian streets in Mayfair.

Turning left at Charles Street, walk towards Red Lion Yard. Opposite The Red Lion is a bottle-green weatherboarded house, perhaps one of the eighteenth-century coach houses built here for the large houses on the Berkeley estate.

At the top of Waverton Street, by St George's School, turn left into South Street walking nearly to Park Lane to find No. 10, the home of Catherine Walters, the last great Victorian courtesan. A child of the Liverpool slums, she was adored by the Prince of Wales, Gladstone and Kitchener. A plaque opposite, between a modern red-brick monstrosity and No. 8, commemorates Florence Nightingale.

Rex Place leads to Mount Street where the American Ambassador J. G. Winant lived in 1941-6. At its east end stands the beautiful Grosvenor Chapel built in 1730. Below a modest green-copper spire, is a deep-blue clockface, with golden hands and golden numerals. John Wilkes, Lady Mary Wortley Montagu and the Duke of Wellington's parents are buried here.

To the left of the Chapel, are the Mount Street Gardens, surrounded by turn-of-the-century flats and at the far end, the Farm Street Church of the Immaculate Conception, headquarters of the English Jesuits. The church was designed in 1844 by Joseph Scoles in decorated Gothic style and the sumptuous interior glitters with gold leaf, malachite, lapis lazuli and red granite.

Leaving the gardens at Carlos Place you pass two traditional butchers, John Bailey and Sons (Poulterers) and R. Allen and Company. Looking through the window you can see the original decorated tiled walls and round freestanding chopping board.

At Davies Street turn left, away from Berkeley Square to Bourdon Street. Bourdon House, now Mallett's, the antique dealers, was built in 1723-5, but has been restored and extended. At the end of King's Yard is an elegant red-brick gatehouse, topped by a copper-domed clock, leading to the Italian Embassy.

Turning right into Brook Street, named after the Tyburn which runs below, you walk past Claridge's, started in 1855 by William Claridge, a butler. South Molton Street, a wonderful place to windowshop for clothes, is on the left. Turn right into Avery Row, stopping to look down Lancashire Court on your left. This tiny old-fashioned yard, hidden from the roar of Oxford Street, contains the headquarters of the campaign to save Avery Row and its surrounds from demolition and Planning Application No. 1895.

Crossing Maddox Street, walk down Bourdon Street, the covered passage opposite. Turn left past the back of Sotheby's to reach New Bond Street. Cross the road to look in the window of Tessier's gold-and silversmiths, founded in 1811 and established on these premises in 1856. At the corner of Grafton Street continue over the pavement and down past Asprey, Cartier, Tiffany and Loewe. On your right is the neo-classical apricot and white stucco entrance to the Royal Arcade opened in 1879.

Retrace your steps to Burlington Arcade (1819), which is lined with shops selling the best wool, gold and chocolate you can buy. The Museum of Mankind on your right was designed by Sir James Pennethorne. It used to belong to the University of London but is now part of the British Museum.

At the beginning of Vigo Street, a plaque on the walls of the Clarendon Gallery tells you that this is where Allen Lane first published his Penguin paperbacks. Turn right into Regent Street and right again through a covered passage into Swallow Street past The Veeraswamy, one of the first Indian restaurants in central London (but not the best), and then past Bentley's Oyster Bar to return to Piccadilly opposite St James's Church.

33 The Monument and Leadenhall

Length: about 1¼ miles. Food: cafés and restaurants in Leadenhall Market. Leadenhall Market is open Monday–Friday, 7 a.m.–4 p.m. Buses: Nos 8A, 15, 21, 25, 35, 40, 43, 44, 47, 48, 133, 501, 510, 513. Underground: Monument.

From the Monument underground station cross Eastcheap and walk down Fish Hill, the old road into London from the south. London Bridge was then further east and you entered the City through the gates by St Magnus the Martyr which you can see at the bottom of the hill. A plaque on the Monument itself tells you about this. Turn left into Monument Street and follow it to the corner of Pudding Lane where a plaque on the corner of Lloyds Bank marks the position of Thomas Faryner's baker's shop, the one that started the Great Fire of 1666.

Head north up Pudding Lane, crossing Eastcheap and continue up Philpot Lane. Cross Fenchurch Street into Lime Street, where lime used to be burnt and sold in the Middle Ages. Towering above the northern end of the street like a twentieth-century spire is Richard Rogers' giant Lloyd's building.

Lime Street bears left past Gieves and Hawkes into Leadenhall Market. Recently refurbished, it's all too clean and the old traders, facing annual rents of £32,000, are threatened by the new caviare, champagne and croissant sellers. But for all that it is a magnificent covered market building. The City's silver gargoyles wag blood red tongues from the top of maroon and cream striped pillars.

Leave the market by the steel and concrete tubular base of the Lloyd's building, walking left around the maze of grids, girders, slots and sheets of glass that scream the importance of Man. Cross Leadenhall Street into the open square. On the right is the church of St Mary Axe, so called because the original church contained one of the legendary axes used by Attila the Hun to murder the Eleven Thousand Virgins, handmaidens of the daughter of the king of England.

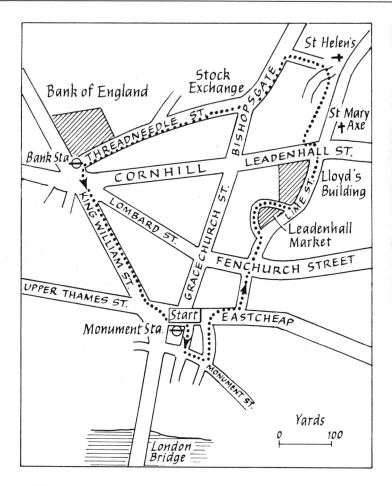

Walking north-east towards a solitary red-brick house amongst soaring office blocks, you find the Church of St Helen of Bishopsgate, now joined with St Martin of Outwich. The double-fronted church is thought to have been built by Constantine on his conversion to Christianity in the fourth century. It contains fifteenth-century choir stalls and seventeenth-century font, pulpit and doorways.

Reaching Bishopsgate via Great St Helen's, you are standing below the neo-classical headquarters of the National Provincial Bank, its statues silhouetted against the black glass windows of the National Westminster Tower. Bearing right at the junction down

Leadenhall Market

Threadneedle Street, you pass on the right the Stock Exchange. On the left outside the Royal Exchange buildings there are benches, a few trees, a fountain and a memorial to Reuter.

At the wide junction of Threadneedle Street, Prince's Street, Poultry, Cornhill, and King William Street, the Bank of England is on your right. The Mansion House stands opposite and in front of the statue of the Duke of Wellington a plaque sets out the landmarks. King William Street leads back to the Monument underground station.

34 Old Chelsea

Length: 2¾ miles. Food: the Cross Keys, Lawrence Street; My Old Dutch, King's Road; Chelsea Farmers' Market, Sydney Street. Carlyle's House is open from Wednesdays to Sundays from April to October, tel. 01–352–7087. Bus: No. 39. Underground: Sloane Square.

From the statue of Thomas Carlyle in Chelsea Embankment Gardens, walk up Cheyne Row past The King's Head and Eight Bells. On the right-hand side of the street Cheyne Cottage is set back from the terrace of red-brick houses built by Lord Cheyne in 1708. Thomas Carlyle lived at No. 24 which is marked with stone bas relief and is open to the public. At the end of the row the late Victorian Church of the Holy Redeemer stands on the site of William de Morgan's warehouse and showroom.

It is tempting to continue north along Glebe Place but save this for later. Instead turn left along Upper Cheyne Row to walk along flagstones beside a pretty terrace of cottages built in about 1840. The Row ends at the top of Lawrence Street, but the cottages continue into a narrow alley beside No. 16 Lawrence Street, a square house on the site of the Chelsea China Factory (1745–84).

Turn left down Lawrence Street, one of the oldest in Chelsea, and turn right again opposite Nos 23 and 24, the Duke's House and Monmouth House, whose two black doors share one portico. Justice Walk, a charming alley, leads to Old Church Street where, turning round you get the best view of Monmouth House.

As you walk into Old Church Street, the oldest street in Chelsea, look to your left where a warehouse has been thoughtfully restored. The iron pulley used for hauling goods up from the street is folded flat above a newly painted blue door.

Walking north towards King's Road you pass No. 46 which has a cow's head peering out of the wall. This was Wright's Dairy, established in 1796. Next door the 1908 dairy building, also with cow's head, has recently been restored. The cows used to graze in fields behind the dairy.

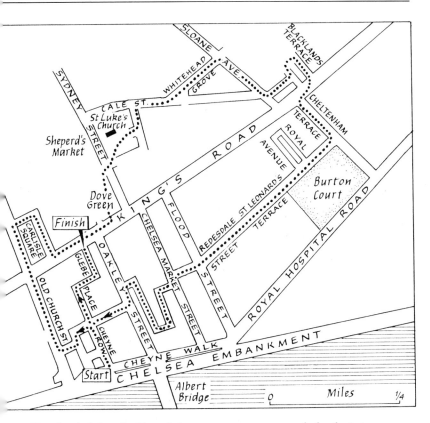

On the left-hand side of the street a narrow arch leads into Hereford Buildings, 1878, once owned by Octavia Hill, housing reformer and founder of the National Trust. The flats used to be rented to elderly women who were treated to an annual outing by Miss Hill. Behind the long brick wall on the right are the Rectory Gardens, now overgrown. If the gate is open you can look at the Rectory where Charles Kingsley lived as a child.

Cross King's Road and continue up Old Church Street. Before turning right at Carlyle Square, if you look further up the street, on the left-hand side you can see the low white buildings of the Chelsea Arts Club which has been here since 1902. Like many of old Chelsea's houses, it has a secret garden behind the wall.

Walk clockwise round Carlyle Square, passing Osbert Sitwell's house (No. 2) before coming back to King's Road. Turn left and walk past the modern Chelsea School of Art and the fire station to the corner of Dovehouse Street. Cross this and bear left over Dovehouse Green to the Chelsea Farmers' Market. The green was a burial ground given to the parish by Hans Sloane and converted in 1977 for the Queen's Silver Jubilee.

The Chelsea Farmers' Market is a relatively new arrival and not a market as such. Nor are there any farmers but there are two Neal's Yard shops (with a steam-driven clock outside) and a selection of expensive grocers. Even better is the white garden furniture arranged on Astroturf outside the café.

Leave the market by the Sydney Street exit and turn left, crossing the road to enter the gardens of St Luke's. The familiar blackened walls of the late Victorian church have recently been cleaned, completely altering the church's personality. Walk behind the church turning right through the stone arch into St Luke's Street.

Turning right into Cale Street, overshadowed by the tall Peabody Buildings on its northern edge, you soon reach Chelsea Green. This minute triangle of grass is all that remains of Chelsea Common. There are some nice shops around here and a particularly good hardware store. Continue over the Green along Whitehead's Grove and turn right into Sloane Avenue. George Seferis, the poet and Greek Ambassador, lived in No. 7, the house at the beginning of Anderson Street.

Turn left along Coulson Street, left again and then right into Blacklands Terrace where you pass John Sandoe's excellent book-shop before reaching King's Road again. Cross the road and turn down Cheltenham Terrace past the Duke of York's Barracks. At the end of the road turn right into St Leonard's Terrace.

On the other side of the road, behind the brick wall, is Burton's Court, a sizeable piece of land that belonged to the Royal Hospital until it was sliced off by Royal Hospital Road. The tall eighteenth-century houses on the right lead to Royal Avenue, a tree-lined gravelled boulevard, intended when built to lead from the Royal Hospital north beyond King's Road. James Bond is supposed to live in one of the overlooking houses.

St Leonard's Terrace leads past the end-of-terrace house on the right, Bram Stoker's house, to Redesdale Street and Alpha Place. As you cross Chelsea Manor Street into Oakley Gardens the gardens get bigger, the trees more plentiful. The Phene Arms stands on the corner of Phene Street leading to Margaretta Terrace.

Cross Oakley Street, the main road to and from Albert Bridge,

Justice Walk meets Lawrence Street

and turn left then right into Upper Cheyne Row. No. 2 is built on the site of Dr Phene's house, built in 1903 and declared to be the most extravagant house in London. It was multi-coloured and heavily decorated; but it lasted only twelve years after the doctor's death in 1912. Nos 16–28 near the church were built in 1716. Leigh Hunt lived in No. 22.

When you reach Glebe Place turn right then right again. Nearly every cottage, studio or house on the southern and eastern sides of Glebe Place is different. It is a wide street and certainly one of the loveliest in Chelsea. The cottages have long roofs almost down to their knees, bas-relief decoration and leafy gardens. There is a modern Italianate building in pale terracotta with copper-green decoration and the eyes of one studio have been closed by a lid of green ivy. Turn right into King's Road past three houses set back from the street behind a brick wall. Ellen Terry and Carol Reid lived in the first two, built in 1720. The third, Argyll House, was designed by the Venetian architect Giacomo Leoni in 1723. Its windows are darkened with neglect while two sheep's skulls stare from the door lintel.

35 Portobello to Golborne Road

Length: 2¼ miles there and back.
Food: 192 Kensington Park Road;
Ceres and the Portobello Coffee
House in Portobello Road; the
Lisboa in Golborne Road. Buses:
Nos 12, 27, 28, 31, 52, 52A, 88.
Underground: Notting Hill Gate.

A bumpy cart track once led through the fields from the Notting Hill turnpike to Portobello Farm. That track is now Portobello Road, one of the liveliest in London and a good walk even when the market crowds have gone.

No one knows exactly when the market started but it was some time round the end of the 1860s and beginning of the 1870s. Originally it was held only on Saturdays and even now, it is only on Fridays and Saturdays that the majority of people turn up. They pour out of Notting Hill Gate underground station and wander up Pembridge Villas in a great snake, changing its skin according to the weather.

Portobello Road changes character continually as it descends Notting Hill, crosses beneath the Great West Road, the Westway, and begins to climb towards Kensal Rise, ending just before the railway line. The first section (up to Chepstow Villas) contains two-up two-down rose-, olive-, terracotta- and lemon-painted cottages with small front gardens. At the end of this early Victorian terrace the stalls begin.

The antique market starts north of Chepstow Villas but the first stalls are the most expensive. Engraved on the end-of-terrace wall on the left is an advertisement for A. Davey, Builder and Manufacturer of every description of inside and outside window blinds, Upholsterer and Decorator est. 1851. Further down the hill on the right is Denbigh Close, leading to Denbigh Mews, a little cobbled alley of stock-brick stables at the end of which stands a brick and stucco gateway. Pretty blue-, grey- and cream-fronted houses slope down towards Westbourne Grove, which on Saturdays is also lined

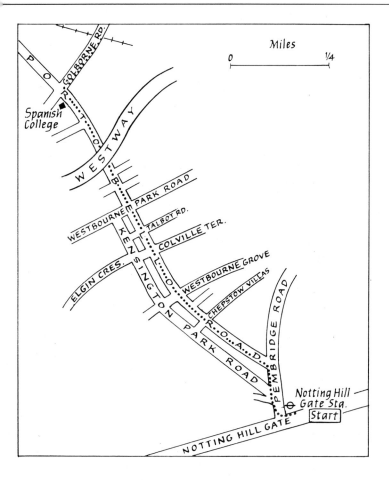

with stalls. W. Jones and Sons' antique arcade at No. 291 on the left used to be a theatre and you can still see the decorative stucco and tiled entrance.

The best of the antiquery is north of Westbourne Grove. Antiques, lace and expensive bric-a-brac are heaped on the stalls and in the arcades. Twenty years ago you could pick up a fiddlephone or a Japanese lacquer chest for a tenner at one of the creaking wooden stalls. Now that might buy a pair of lace bloomers, but you'd have to bargain. Round about here you'll find the organgrinder with his blue macaw.

The fruit and vegetable market starts at the junction with Elgin

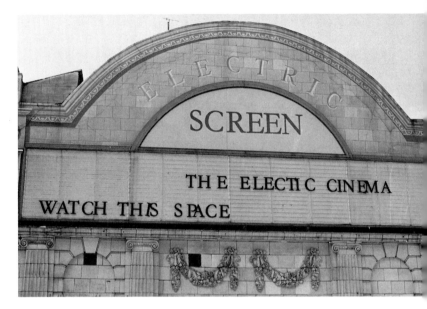

SCREEN

THE ELECTIC CINEMA

WATCH THIS SPACE

Under threat

Crescent where there are some excellent shops: Graham and Green for presents, Elgin Books, Mr Christian's delicatessen. If you're looking for fruit and vegetables, walk on a bit before buying. The shops on the left-hand side of the road sell clothes, from punk to ethnic, while those on the right are more domestic. Look out on the left for the Electric Cinema, the earliest purpose-built cinema in London, which has been empty for some time and is in constant danger of being turned into a nightclub or something equally appalling.

Portobello is a muddle of colour and noise. Dodge jettisoned onions and bruised bananas lying in the gutter. Jump up on the pavement to avoid the occasional car foolish enough to try driving through the sea of people. The smell of German sausages grilled outside in a mobile hut threads through the crowds. Outside the pubs dope deals are made with sleight of hand.

Approaching the Westway – that ugly slash of concrete overhead that has left the people who live here still trying to heal the wound – the fruit and vegetables are replaced by cheap clothes, the new and garish, old and faded. Secondhand jeans, secondhand fridges – look for long enough and you can find anything except livestock. There are many places to eat, some of which are listed above.

The local Spanish people go to the Spanish College at the junction of Portobello and Golborne Roads where stalls spill on to the tarmac. People can hire stalls for £12, payable at the end of the day, and sell their belongings to pay the rent.

Turn right into Golborne Road, which is wide but only just enough to cope with all the stalls and trestle tables. The Golborne Road church on the left is a pretty white and blue building set into a Victorian terrace of shops, including some interesting antique shops.

Over the last few years, the opening of contemporary art and photography galleries has given the whole area a real shot in the arm. And with the Portobello arts festival now established annually it's only getting better all the time.

36 Soho

Length: about 1½ miles round trip.
Food: Andrew Edmonds Wine
Bar in Lexington Street; Patisserie
Valerie in Old Compton Street;
Maison Bertaux in Greek Street;
Poon's in Lisle Street. The House
of St Barnabas is open on Wed-
nesdays, 2.30–4.15 p.m. and
Thursdays, 11 a.m.–12.30 p.m.
Buses: Nos 3, 6, 9, 12, 13, 14, 15,
19, 22, 22B, 38, 53, 88. Under-
ground: Piccadilly Circus.

This is one of the best central London areas to walk around; cars have a hellish fight squeezing through the narrow streets. Soho was built up on farmland in the 1670s and 1680s as thousands of immigrants settled here. Four centuries later continents of cooking smells hang in Soho's airless passages.

From the mayhem of Piccadilly Circus walk up Sherwood Street past the cake-white walls of the Regent Palace Hotel. Brewer Street was developed in the 1670s and named after the breweries which stood on its north side. The street is lined with the sandwich bars, restaurants, film and production studios, clothes shops and sex shops that fill the streets of Soho.

Turn left into Great Pulteney Street, named after William Pulteney, who owned the land round here. Ahead lies Beak Street and a late eighteenth-century terrace built of stock brick, now darkened with grime. The house at the top of the street has been given an untidy Victorian façade with dollops of stucco and Corinthian columns. On the right-hand corner with Beak Street stands a rather lovely building of 1905 decorated with green-glazed bricks.

Turn right into Beak Street and left into Lexington Street past Andrew Edmonds' black-fronted eighteenth-century print shop and wine bar (No. 46). Between the two is an old-fashioned stone-flagged courtyard which you can see from the street when the door is open.

Broadwick Street was built between 1686 and 1736. William Blake was born at No. 74; Harpers and Queen is at the narrow west end. At its east end, originally called Broad Street, is the beginning of Berwick Street market which has been going since the eighteenth

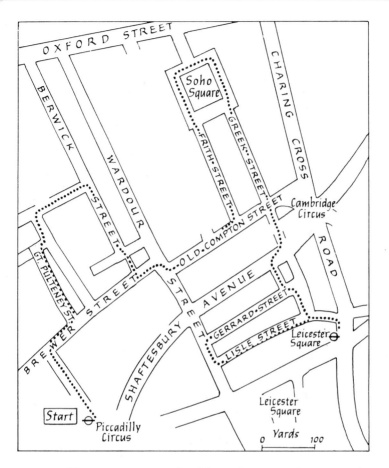

century. There are some early eighteenth-century houses on its eastern side and The Blue Posts pub at No. 22 has been there in name since 1739. The market itself is open daily, except on Sundays. A noisy, battling crowd of locals swells the street and the stalls specialise in fruit and vegetables. On the left-hand corner with Peter Street is a traditional Italian grocer's, Fratelli Camisa, which smells of Italy.

The market continues in Rupert Street, on the other side of Walker Court, above which flash the red neon lights of Raymond's Revue Bar. Continue along Brewer Street and turn right into Wardour Street, named after another local landowner Edward Wardour. A map of 1585 shows that this used to be called

Commonhedge Lane, leading from the Uxbridge Road, now Oxford Street, to the King's Mews, now Trafalgar Square. Sheraton lived at Nos 103 and 147 but it is the film industry who have ruled since the 1930s. A little way down on your left are the small gardens of Queen Anne's Church of which only the tower remains. This is unfortunately in the car park behind the hoardings.

Back-track to Old Compton Street to I. Camisa & Son, the grocer, and A. Moroni and Son's newsstand, famous for its international supply of newspapers: the *Irish Times* and *New York Times* are both on sale. By the end of the eighteenth century Old Compton Street was Soho's main shopping street. It was also a favourite with the French; Rimbaud and Verlaine used to meet here for a drink.

The Algerian Coffee Stores at No. 52 sells marvellous coffee and just across Dean Street, at No. 44, is Patisserie Valerie with a comfortable, darkened interior where you can eat the best French cakes.

Turn left up Frith Street to walk towards Soho Square. Richard Frith was a bricklayer who built the first houses in Soho Square. Ronnie Scott's is on your left. Further along, on the same side of the street, is a small Victorian pub, The Dog and Duck with its original glazed-tile wall, wooden bar and tiled entrance. Hazlitt's house at No. 6 on the right-hand side near the square was built in 1718. The three stock-brick Georgian house with sober black front doors is now a hotel.

Soho Square is surrounded by individual houses, the first of which were built in the seventeenth century. An engraving of 1731 shows forty-one houses around a square of four neat clipped lawns, then known as King Square, the land having belonged to Charles II. Only No. 10 and No. 15 remain from that period. A statue of the king by Caius Gabriel Cibber has stood in the square since 1681. In the 1780s some of the smartest families moved to Mayfair and their houses were bought by foreign diplomats, MPs and professional men. Office development in the 1920s and '30s dramatically altered the square's appearance. The pseudo-Elizabethan black and white timber toolshed in the garden was put there in the 1870s.

Leave the square by Greek Street, which was named after the Greek Orthodox church that stood in Hog Lane. No. 1, The House of Barnabas, built in the 1740s, is now a temporary home for women. The rococo interior is one of the finest in London. Wedgwood's

Chinese herbalist in Lisle Street

London showrooms were at Nos 12–13 and Thomas de Quincey rented rooms here in 1802.

From the start there have been inns, coffee houses and warehouses in Greek Street. Today No. 3 is Milroy's the malt whiskey specialists, L'Escargot is at No. 48, and south of Old Compton Street is Maison Bertaux.

The Chinese have adopted the slice of Soho on the south side of Shaftesbury Avenue. Walk down Gerrard Street, once lived in by John Dryden, David Wilkie, George Morland, John Cotman and James Boswell. In the 1920s and '30s there were nightclubs; strip joints in the '50s. A few years ago Westminster Council put up scarlet and gold pagodas, dragon gates, pagoda telephone kiosks and street signs in Chinese and English.

Turn right into Lisle Street to find a jumble of Chinese supermarkets in a Victorian brick terrace. Poon's wind-dry restaurant is followed by the Chinese herbalist Po Sau Tong whose window is filled with forty-six sweet jars of sliced, dried bundles of seeds, pods, nuts and organic matter. Engraved in the pediment on the central house in the terrace is the date 1791. St John's Hospital for

Diseases of the Skin decorated with stepped gables, was built in the 1890s.

Rupert Street is lined with Chinese restaurants. Look down Rupert Court, a narrow alley with a house built over the arch at the far end. The 'Ancient Lights' sign prevents it from any building that might block its light. Turn right off Rupert Street back into Gerrard Street, which you walk along to reach Newport Court and Leicester Square underground.

37 Southwark

Length: about 1¼ miles one way.
Food: The Borough Café, Park
Street. The Shakespeare Globe
Museum is open Monday–Satur-
day 10 a.m.–5 p.m. Sundays 1.30–
5.30 p.m. Tel. 01–928–6342.
Buses: Nos 6, 9, 11, 15, 15A, 17,
76, 95, 149, 184, 513. Under-
ground: Mansion House, Cannon
Street, Monument.

This walk is best done early on a weekday morning when Borough
Market is open – seven-thirty is a good time. Start from Southwark
Bridge, cross on the west side and walk down the first set of steps to
Bankside, a cobbled lane running beside the Thames. Buried
beneath the cobbles are the corpses of the whores who worked the
popular sixteenth-century brothels here. Across the river stands St

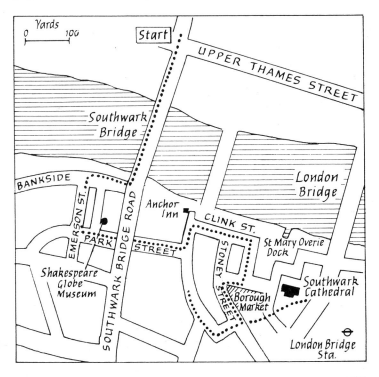

Paul's behind a row of warehouses, most of them modern red brick –
only one, painted white, remains from the last century. The white-
painted wooden embankment you're standing beside might not last
long in the great scrum of building going on round here. And
because of the building be prepared to adapt the route given here.

Take the second turning away from the river up Emerson Street.
Turn left into Park Street and immediately left again into Bear
Gardens. On the left-hand side are two attractive warehouses: Porn
and Dunwoody engineers and the Union Works. The Shakespeare
Globe Museum is in the converted eighteenth-century warehouse
opposite, pockmarked with pale brick where there used to be more
windows. Inside is a replica of an early seventeenth-century theatre.
This is the site of the Davies Amphitheatre, famous for dog fighting
and bear and bull baiting, popular in Britain from the twelfth until
the seventeenth century and not officially banned until 1835.

Walk back to Park Street and turn left past Rose Alley, the site of
the Rose Theatre, the first playhouse in Bankside, built in 1586–7.
Continue along Park Street under Southwark Bridge Road past the
end of Horse Shoe Alley and turn left up Bank End. The famous
Anchor Inn, built in 1775, overlooks the river. Its charm has been
destroyed by heavy-handed restoration – varnish on the wooden
shutters and glitzy signs, plus the kind of outdoor seating area you
find in a motorway service station.

At the corner of Clink Street, beside the Clink Street Vaults wine
shippers' warehouses, walk through the brick-vaulted tunnel under
the railway line. The Clink, in Clink Street, was the medieval prison,
in use until burnt down in the Gordon Riots in 1780. This narrow
and dark alley leads between tall, grimy warehouses, lit in the early
morning by a rare slice of yellow light.

The alley leads to Pickfords Wharf, restored recently, and
noticeably, with yellow brick. On the right, hidden until you're
actually beside it, is the fourteenth-century rose window from the
Bishop of Winchester's Palace, discovered in a warehouse after a fire
in 1814. The palace was built in 1109 and its seventy-acre parkland
estate was known as the Liberty of the Clink, being outside the
jurisdiction of the City. This had its advantages. Far from objecting
to the local whoring, the Bishops fixed the rules and the tarts became
known as the Bishops of Winchester's geese.

Moored in St Mary Overie Dock is the *Kathleen & May*, a trading
schooner built in 1900 and now open to visitors. The Old Thame-

Cannon Street station's towers from St Mary Overie

side Inn on the left has nothing old about it, but it does have seating outside by the river and an excellent view of Cannon Street station.

Turn left off Winchester Walk into Stoney Street past sooty Victorian warehouses, and walk under the railway bridge to Borough Market. Early in the morning boxes of steaming freshly boiled beets stand waiting for a yellow forklift truck to move them to the buyer's van. Sacks of potatoes from Norfolk and crates of Suffolk spinach lie in the damp cabbage-smelling streets and in the mid-nineteenth-century covered market.

Turn right into Park Street, which belonged to Thomas Cure, saddler to Queen Elizabeth, and has changed little since it was rebuilt in 1881.

Turn back to walk through the market to Cathedral Street and Southwark Cathedral, the Cathedral Church of St Saviour and St Mary Overie. It is the fourth church on this site and a cathedral since 1905. This church, built in 1220, is the oldest Gothic-style church in London and parts of the earlier Norman Priory church can still be seen inside. Climb the steps from the cathedral up to London Bridge and walk across it to reach the Monument underground.

38 St James's

Length: about 1¼ miles. Food: La   25, 38, 55. Underground: Green
Bonbonniere, Duke Street St   Park.
James's. Buses: Nos 9, 14, 19, 22,

Turn right out of the southern exit of Green Park underground and
turn right again before the Ritz. A wide tarmac path runs downhill
between the park and the backs of large houses. Walk down this,
turning left into Milkmaid's Passage which leads to the Stable Yard
of St James's Palace. As you turn right, which you have to do as the
other roads are private, you can see Ambassador's Court, one of the
four courts at St James's, the others being the Friary, Engine and
Colour Courts. The palace was built by Henry VIII and restored in
1814 after fire broke out. As you walk down Stable Yard Road to the
Mall you pass Clarence House where the Queen Mother lives.

Turn left into the Mall, crossing Marlborough Road to walk
before the squat fluted columns of Nash's Carlton House Terrace.
Nash had been asked to design terraces to go all round St James's
Park, but these two 31-bay-wide terraces were the only ones built. At
the end of the first terrace turn left and march up the steps of the
monument to the Grand Old Duke of York.

Walk alongside Carlton Gardens, the small shady garden on the
right. Curzon lived at No. 1 Carlton Gardens, Kitchener at No. 2,
Palmerston at No. 4. In the north-western corner of the gardens is a
statue of Robert Falcon Scott next to a row of cast-iron gas braziers
standing in front of what used to be the United Services Club.
Opposite stands the Athenaeum, square and white stucco, with
Roman Doric pillars supporting the porch. A gilded figure of Pallas
Athene. The frieze running above the main windows was adapted
from that on the Parthenon. Designed by Decimus Burton in 1828–
30, the club's members include prime ministers, cabinet ministers,
archbishops and bishops.

Turn left off Waterloo Place, which once swept forward to
Carlton House and into Pall Mall and was the ancient route from the
City to St James's Palace. On the left-hand side you pass The

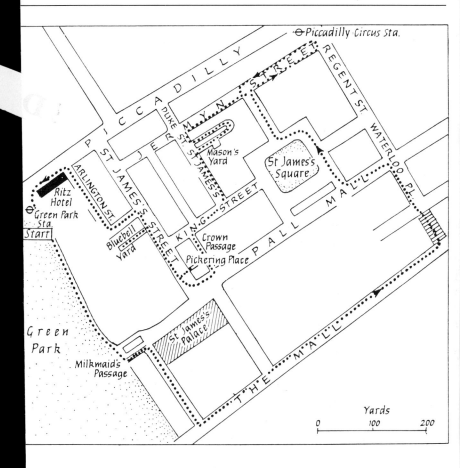

Travellers' and The Reform Clubs. When the Prince Regent lived at Carlton House, St James's was a gentleman's paradise.

Cross the road into St James's Square, passing a plaque marking Norfolk House where Eisenhower planned and launched Operations Torch and Overlord which liberated NW Africa and NW Europe in the Second World War. At the end of Charles II Street you can see the Haymarket Theatre designed by John Nash. Continue anti-clockwise round the square past No. 4, built in 1676 and the home of Nancy Astor. Just before leaving the square, you should look at the two houses in the corner: No. 14, built in 1896, contains the London Library and Nos 9–10, built in 1736, are

145

Chatham House, the home of the Royal Institute of International Affairs. William Pitt, Edward Stanley and William Gladstone all lived in No. 10.

Walking up Duke of York Street you can see the grey-painted octagonal clocktower of St James's. Turn right into Jermyn Street which until recently was one of the few streets with shops that catered only for men. Now the shirtmakers drape their shirts over female busts and sell striped shirts with frilly collars.

The houses built by Henry Jermyn, Earl of St Albans, in the 1680s have now all gone. Astleys at No. 109 are briar pipe specialists established in 1862. Rowley's Restaurant where Thomas Wall, ice-cream maker, was born in 1846, is at No. 113.

At the junction with Regent Street cross to the north side and walk back along Jermyn Street past Trumper's Gentlemen's Hairdresser at No. 20. Inside the polished shelves are arranged with bristle shaving brushes, real sponges and bottles of gentlemen's preparations. Bates, the hatters, founded in 1900, with its window full of traditional men's hats is at No. 21A and in Eagle Place to the right you'll find Landaw's snuff shop. Continuing past the back of Simpson's, cross the road again to look at Paxton and Whitfield, established in 1740 by a Suffolk cheesemonger. Below the black and brass shop sign the window display is mouthwatering. Inside there is a vast selection of cheeses and best-quality groceries. Floris, the perfumers, are next door. Cross the road again to wander through Princes Arcade, a covered Victorian shopping arcade. Opposite its entrance No. 87 stands on the site of Isaac Newton's house. Next door is Jules Bar, originally known as the Waterloo Hotel, which has stood on this site since the beginning of the last century.

At the corner of Duke Street St James's turn left and walk downhill, looking at the paintings in the windows of the many galleries lining the street, a constantly changing free art gallery. Turn left up Mason's Yard, walking round the cobbled yard back to Duke Street where you turn left to find La Bonbonniere. Squeezed between stern four-storey art galleries, this little café seems under constant threat. One day someone is bound to come along and knock it down so they can build another four-storey giant.

Turn right into King Street and cross the road to walk down Crown Passage, dark and narrow, lined with local shops, sandwich bars, a newsstand, an ironmonger and lit by wall-mounted gas lamps. No. 18, a dark, green-shuttered shop, is the back of Lock and Co.

Mason's Yard meets Duke Street

The passage leads to Pall Mall, at the corner of St James's Street where you turn right.

Just after Berry Bros and Rudd Ltd, wine merchants established in the seventeenth century, turn right into a half-timbered passage, Pickering Place. A plaque on the wall commemorates the meeting of the Texan legation here in 1842–5. The passage leads to a small stone-flagged courtyard surrounded by brick houses and more gas lamps. The houses were built in 1730 by William Pickering whose mother-in-law ran the grocer's shop from which Berry Bros started.

Walking up the magnificently wide St James's Street, stop to look back at the Palace. You pass Lock and Co., the hatters with the same green paint, the paint thickened with the passing years and layers. Next is Lobb's the bootmaker. In striking contrast is Credit Suisse's steel and black-glass tubular building on your left and opposite it The Economist building (1966–8). Opposite King Street is the Palladian Carlton Club. On the west side of the street, turn down Blue Ball Yard where 1741 coach houses have been preserved as garages. Black iron steps lead up to the tiled cottages, each of which is hung with baskets of flowers, while tubs line the steps.

Return to St James's Street, and walk to Brooks's yellow brick and stone building designed by Henry Holland in 1778 which stands on the corner of Park Place. Opposite is Boodle's, built in 1765. White's, the oldest of these London clubs, is the white house, built 1778 with a bow window (1811) at the top of St James's Street, on the right. About fifty yards down Park Place walk up the pale yellow stone steps on the right which lead to Arlington Street where you walk past the entrance to the Ritz and back to Piccadilly.

39 St Paul's and Blackfriars

Length: about 1¼ miles one way.
Food: AA Restaurant in Carter
Lane. Buses: Nos 6, 9, 11, 15,
15A, 17, 76, 95, 149, 184, 513.
Underground: Mansion House.

To reach the beginning of the walk from the underground, head east along Queen Victoria Street and turn left down Lambeth Hill to cross Upper Thames Street using the overpass. There are so many roads and such an amount of new construction that it's not particularly pleasant. At the end of High Timber, follow Trig Lane to the riverfront opposite Bankside power station at Southwark, designed by George Gilbert Scott. You are now standing at the bottom of a long flight of pale yellow stone steps that lead up to a magnificent view of the grey dome of St Paul's Cathedral. As you climb the steps between the red-brick City of London School and a

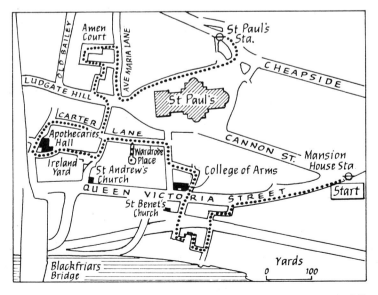

pink granite office block, the dome recedes and the body of the church fills the view.

Before crossing Upper Thames Street into Peters Hill, turn left to find St Benet's. This is the only red-brick church Wren built. Small and square, it is decorated with white stone quoins and, again unusual for Wren, carved swags of flowers above the arched windows. Services are in Welsh as this is the London church of the Welsh Episcopalians. Almost opposite stands the 1678 College of Arms, responsible for heraldry and pageantry.

At the top of the steps of Peters Hill, turn left into Knightrider Court. Turn right past the Horn Tavern into Godliman Street and left into Carter Lane and the Blackfriars conservation area. Until the last century Carter Lane was called Shoemaker Row because the cobblers worked here.

The AA Restaurant on the corner with Dean's Court has its original 1930s frosted glass and cream-coloured exterior. Just up Dean's Court on the left is an example of one of the grand houses built after the Great Fire. The Old Deanery, six bays wide, was designed by Wren in 1670. Behind the wall a patterned cobblestone courtyard leads to a double staircase to the front door.

On the corner of Dean's Court and Carter Lane is a youth hostel, a ~~beautiful~~ Victorian building of yellow brick, decorated with stone ~~_ and a frieze. Just after the tiled row of houses in Addle Hill, ~~first~~ mentioned in the thirteenth century, a covered passage on the left leads into Wardrobe Place.

This oval courtyard is cobbled and shaded with trees. It was built at the beginning of the eighteenth century on the site of the Gardens of the King's Wardrobe. The Wardrobe was a house given to Edward III where he stored his clothes as well as ceremonial dress and all accoutrements for courtiers, ambassadors etc. The royal household did this until the Wardrobe was destroyed in the Great Fire. On the right, Nos 3 and 5 have survived from the 1800s.

Returning to Carter Street, turn left down St Andrew's Hill past No. 36 which has a lovely narrow door at the end and two square letterboxes set into the railings outside. Next door St Andrew's House has its original wrought-iron lamp holder. Straight ahead through the iron gate is St Andrew-by-the-Wardrobe, the last church Wren built.

Wardrobe Place meets Addle Hill

Turn right beside The Cockpit down Ireland Yard, a narrow passage running parallel with Carter Street. Up a short flight of stone steps on the right is Ireland Yard, a quiet, leafy churchyard that belonged to St Ann's Blackfriars which was destroyed in the Great Fire and never rebuilt. Beside the steps is a fragment of the wall of the Dominican priory, Blackfriars Monastery.

The Blackfriars Playhouse stood in Playhouse Yard until 1655. In 1613 Shakespeare bought a house in this area for £140. Turn right at the end of the yard into Blackfriars Lane which leads past the Apothecaries' Hall, built in 1688 by Thomas Locke. Looking through the arched passage into the courtyard you can see in the centre an elegant wrought-iron lampstand and behind it on the wall a copper pestle and mortar.

Turn right into Carter Lane, at the corner of which a blue plaque marks the site of Blackfriars Monastery. Recent excavations carried out north of Carter Lane (on the site of Nos 55–56) revealed a Norman ditch, which surrounded the Norman Montfichet Tower built inside the medieval city walls.

Turn left up Creed Lane and bear left into Ludgate Hill. Cross the road to walk along Stationer's Hall Court to Stationers' Hall, built in 1673, refronted in 1800 and restored after bombing in 1940. Turn left under the modern buildings to reach the southern entrance to Amen Court, built after the Great Fire. Follow the Court round to the main gateway on to Ave Maria Lane. Turn right and then left behind St Paul's Cathedral to the underground station.

40 The Temple to Lincoln's Inn Fields

Length: nearly 1¼ miles one way.
Food: The Devereux Arms in
Devereux Court; Gloriette Patisserie in High Holborn. Soane
Museum: open Tues.–Sat. 10
a.m.–5 p.m. Buses: Nos 59, 109,
184. Underground: Temple.

This is a walk not to be hurried. Leaving Temple underground
station you can avoid the noisy Embankment by walking left through
Temple Gardens which bring you out on Temple Place and back on
the Embankment at the entrance to the City of London.

From wrought-iron gates on the Embankment, through the
decorative Victorian gateway, you finally reach Middle Temple Lane
which rises timelessly up the hill. The soot-stained red-brick
buildings lining Middle Temple Lane exude the same authority as
their occupants like to. As you walk up the hill, stop at the Middle
Temple Treasury Office on the left and ask at the Secretary's Office
on the ground floor for a map of the Temple.

The piece of land known as the Temple is named after the Order
of the Knights Templar, founded in 1118 to protect pilgrims
journeying to the Holy City. Henry I brought the Templars to
England and to London where they had settled on this site by the
twelfth century. In 1308, the vast wealth, power and pride of the
Templars lead to their downfall and brutal suppression. In 1324 the
Templars' London property was handed over to their rivals the
Knights Hospitaller, who allowed lawyers and students lodgings
here. After the destruction of the Hospitallers in 1539, James I
granted the freehold of the land in 1608 to the two societies of
lawyers, known as the Benchers of the Inner Temple and Middle
Temple.

Walking through the arch halfway up Middle Temple Lane, you
enter the Inner Temple whose insignia is Pegasus. The green lawns
of Inner Temple Gardens, seen through the closed iron gates
(1730), were where what we now call the Chelsea Flower Show used

153

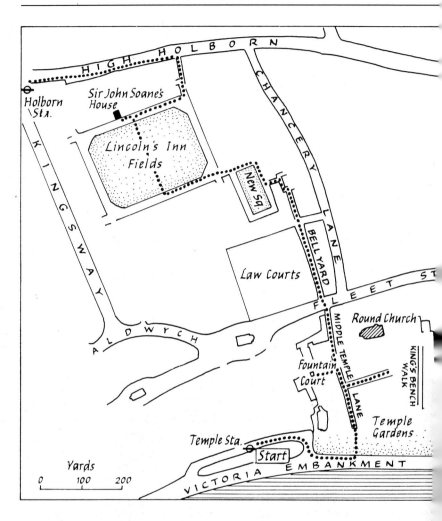

to be held. A flight of steps on your left lead up to the Templars' refectory, behind which is their beautiful ochre-coloured stone Round Church, consecrated in 1185. The rectangular choir was added in 1204. The whole is known as the Temple Church. Around the walls of the Round Church, its roof supported by columns of mottled green Purbeck marble, hideous gargoyles gape and grimace.

Passing under the west porch and the heavy Norman doorway, you reach a small graveyard in the shade of young London planes. Having looked at Hare Court and Dr Johnson's Buildings, wander

154

up Inner Temple Lane to the half-timbered gateway on to Fleet Street. Heading back down King's Bench Walk cross Middle Temple Lane to Fountain Court.

The fountain is a single jet of water that breaks the smooth surface of a neat circular pond. Resting on one of the wooden benches in the shadow of the few trees, you can watch the black-figured barristers about their business. To the south, Middle Temple Gardens stretch down to the Thames. Up a flight of steps to New Court, wrought-iron gates lead to Devereux Court and The Devereux. The 1667 arch in the buildings opposite lead into Essex Court where Oliver Goldsmith and John Evelyn lived.

Go back to Middle Temple Lane and walk through the gateway on to Fleet Street, straight over into Bell Yard, named after the Bell Inn which stood in Carey Lane. Dickens came here whilst writing *David Copperfield.*

Cross Carey Street into Star Yard at the corner of an eighteenth-century house occupied by the Solicitors' Disciplinary Tribunal. Just before Chichester Rents is a urinal, perhaps Victorian, maybe earlier, made of decorated cast iron and painted green.

Lawyers' lair in New Square

At the end of Star Yard, Bishop's Court Gate leads into Lincoln's Inn and New Square. Founded in the middle of the fourteenth century, this is the oldest of the four Inns of Court. The low Old Buildings on your right were built between 1524 and 1613. The Chapel is an early example of seventeenth-century Gothic, probably designed by Inigo Jones. John Donne laid the foundation stone.

Lincoln's Inn is brighter and more open than the Temple with lower buildings less densely arranged. Perhaps the presence of Lincoln's Inn Fields to the north, the largest square in London, adds to this feeling of lightness. Purse Field and Cup Field, used for play by Lincoln's Inn students since the fourteenth century, are now rather bedraggled. Perhaps the Fields will always be desolate. Robberies, murders and executions have all happened here. It became more civilised by 1641 when the houses were built, but even so Lord William Russell was beheaded here in 1683 for his part in the Rye House Plot. A plaque in the bandstand at the middle of the Fields is thought to mark the spot.

From the gate at the northern side of the Fields cross the street to reach John Soane's House at No. 13, one of only two of the original houses left. (The other is Lindsay House, Nos 57–58.) Soane's House is open to visitors and is one of the most fascinating museums in London. Soane began life in 1753 as a bricklayer's son with no 'e' at the end of his name. He became a successful architect, married an heiress and added the 'e'. In 1788 he became architect to the Bank of England, Professor of Architecture at the Royal Academy in 1806 and soon after moved into No. 13 Lincoln's Inn Fields.

The house remains as he left it with his fabulous collections of busts, bronzes, books, paintings (eight scenes from Hogarth's *Rake's Progress*) and assorted antique fragments. These hang above doors, on walls, stand in niches, outside and inside the house and in the mystical Monk's Parlour, yard and cell. Do allow plenty of time to see everything. Before his death in 1837 Sir John, as he had become, managed to secure his home as a public museum by an Act of Parliament.

Leave Lincoln's Inn Fields on the north-east, where Turnstile Row leads on to High Holborn and the underground.

Further Information

These are by no means all those that I have consulted, but they are the most generally useful guides, in the order:

Andrew Crowe, *The Parks and Woodlands of London*, Fourth Estate, 1987. An invaluable guide to all the open spaces in London.

Ed. Christopher Hibbert and Ben Weinreb, *The London Encyclopaedia*, Macmillan, 1987. Encyclopedic information about nearly every street, place and area of London.

Blue Guide to London, A. & C. Black, 1986.

Michelin Green Guide to London.

Ed. David Perrott, *Ordnance Survey Guide to the River Thames*, Nicholson, 1984.

Citisights of London, 145 Goldsmith's Row, London E2 8QR, tel. 01–739–2372/4853, offer a large range of walks into London's past, guided by archaeologists and historians.

Leaflets about local walks are often compiled by members of the Ramblers Association. For details contact their headquarters at 1/5 Wandsworth Road, London SW8 2XX, tel. 01–582–6878.

Acknowledgements

Thank you Kevin Flude of Citisights of London, my guide through the maze of streets in the City of London and without whom the City walks would never have been so easily done. Thank you also Laura, Bernie and Jake, who got soaked and nearly missed their Sunday lunch showing me the giant in Hadley Wood.

Index